ort
as
rd,
He
as
or

By the same author

NOVELS

Pack of Lies
Heaven
Shirker

STORIES

The Man Who Wasn't Feeling Himself

ELECTRIC

CHAD TAYLOR

JONATHAN CAPE
LONDON

F101 586

£15·13

Published by Jonathan Cape 2003

2 4 6 8 10 9 7 5 3 1

First published in Great Britain in 2003 by
Jonathan Cape
Random House, 20 Vauxhall Bridge Road,
London SW1V 2SA

Random House Australia (Pty) Limited
20 Alfred Street, Milsons Point, Sydney,
New South Wales 2061, Australia

Random House New Zealand Limited
18 Poland Road, Glenfield,
Auckland 10, New Zealand

Random House (Pty) Limited
Endulini, 5A Jubilee Road, Parktown 2193, South Africa

The Random House Group Limited Reg. No. 954009
www.randomhouse.co.uk

A CIP catalogue record for this book
is available from the British Library

ISBN 0–224–06926–8

Papers used by Random House are natural,
recyclable products made from wood grown in sustainable forests;
the manufacturing processes conform to the environmental
regulations of the country of origin

Typeset by Deltatype Ltd, Birkenhead, Merseyside

Printed and bound in Great Britain by
Biddles Ltd, King's Lynn and Guildford

For the gang

Power failure shuts down New Zealand's largest city

24 February 1998

AUCKLAND, New Zealand (CNN)

A power blackout that shut down most of New Zealand's largest city has continued into its fifth day.

Auckland has been dark since Friday when three of the four main power cables running into the central business district failed, cutting electricity to downtown offices and more than 5,000 apartments.

It is not known what caused the cables to fail, and experts say it may take up to a year to find out.

Power company officials say a temporary overhead cable will be connected by Monday, boosting the available amount of power to 50% of normal levels.

However there is no guarantee that this cable will not also fail.

(Associated Press and Reuters contributed to this report.)

<u>Unidentified corpse found</u>
24 February 1998
AUCKLAND, New Zealand
Item 3, Channel 3, 6 p.m. broadcast

Police have yet to identify the victim of a
fatal shooting found in central Auckland early
this morning.

The body of the male, described as European by
police, was discovered in an unlocked vehicle
by security personnel during the city's
blackout.

Police are still searching for the murder
weapon. They have appealed to the public for
information.

I

They Say It's Wonderful

Chapter 1

I was overtaking on the inside when the wheel went up on the metal and I lost control and the car spun out, spinning back across until it slammed into the motorway bridge that had been a long way ahead last time I looked but was now suddenly filling the windscreen. And then, just as fast, the driver's compartment was dusty with snowflakes of breaking glass and an enormous noise of twisting and tearing metal, and the car folded like a paper cup.

The accident backed up traffic for miles. The cop in pursuit hit his siren and started reversing down the shoulder to warn other vehicles but they were already coming to a stop as fast as he could back past them. I was watching my blood pool in the broken wing mirror and feeling the inertia spreading outwards from the crumpled saloon like shock waves, slowing everything down, bringing it all into focus.

I remember the oxygen mask being put over my face and then everything started to feel smooth and all right. The firemen used the big pneumatic cutters to open the roof and slide me out. The paramedics cut away my clothes and then I was naked in the white sheets, bare and bleeding, and the ambulance was travelling as fast as I had been when I lost my grip on the steering.

When they wheeled me into the hospital I had a split liver and head trauma and a broken right shoulder, arm, elbow and right ankle. I was conscious going into the theatre. I knew I was going to be okay because the worst was over: I was in the clear.

And then someone phoned in the licence plate and registration and traced not my name, Samuel Usher, but the car's owner, my girlfriend, Dr Alice Mills: a resident intensivist at the same hospital where I was being spread out on the operating table like so much meat.

One of the nurses called Alice but she didn't answer the phone, so they sent someone round to find her near comatose in our bed, the onyx side table noisy with powders and prescription drugs she'd signed out herself from the hospital pharmacy.

Of the two of us, Alice was the first to regain consciousness, the first to sober up and realise what had happened. They had discovered what we'd been doing and it was over: her career, us, everything. I took much longer to catch on.

Alice and I met two years before when I was having one of those colds that don't go away. She made house calls if you knew the right people, which I did. Dr Alice Mills charged three figures plus the fare for the taxi which she kept running downstairs with the meter going while she looked you over. She was pale with a slight overbite and calm, grey eyes and fine hands that travelled across my face and chest like someone skim-reading a page.

There was nothing in my body she hadn't seen before. She depressed my tongue and asked if it was speed or coke and I nodded: yes and yes, and yes to everything else she didn't need to say. My nose was bleeding. I was having palpitations. Maybe an irregular heartbeat. She said there was a bad shipment doing the rounds. I said I could have told her that. She said I should get hold of some good stuff and wrote me a scrip for a fuck-off decongestant that knocked everything out in twenty-four hours. I paid in cash. I asked to see her again and she smiled when I said it. She smiled a lot. When I first met Alice, she was a very happy person.

When we moved in together I wanted to get a bigger TV and a dog but instead we spent our money on a stereo and swapping a lot of her records over to CD. I sat through a couple of recitals before I got her into jazz. I taught her how to count through *Nefertiti*, late Coltrane. I like modal jazz, the way the players race through the songs, but she liked the softer stuff. She liked Johnny Hartman singing falling in love is wonderful. She had been at Auckland Hospital for eighteen months when we got our place, and she had dispensing authority.

I only saw the pharmaceutical supply room once. It was a large, walk-in cupboard with a combination lock on the door and shelves that reached the ceiling with every kind of drip, pill, solution and powder imaginable. She could name them all – I knew them by their effect. It doesn't matter what a phial or capsule is called. All that matters is what happens when you take it. Acceleration, slow motion, cold, warmth, relaxation: it could all be signed out on the doctor's authority.

Alice covered up for it by changing the numbers for other patients here and there. As long as the numbers added up, nobody checked. People trusted her. She kept long hours. She worked hard.

Because Alice never fucked up. She helped a lot of people and she saved lives. She gurgled with dumb, muted pleasure while we kissed and groggily fucked. She held my hand. She brought new things home to try. She introduced me to her friends.

I didn't have much in common with her crowd. I was writing statistical reports while most of her friends were in medicine or hard-core research. To them, I was just some guy messing with numbers. Not that they didn't care about her, or know what we got up to when we were out of sight. A few of her colleagues had been there and others were headed in that direction. The distance between thinking about it and doing it was no thicker than a manila envelope.

Alice had a soft, singsong way of speaking. At work she would chat to her colleagues about gardening or old Hollywood movies or Chinese music – things either everybody knew or nobody would have thought of. Her cheerfulness was deliberate. It put her above the others by making her responsibilities seem easily won, but the competition wasn't to psych other people out. The competition was within herself. She wanted to go as deep as she could and still come out smiling. She wanted to be as carefree as anyone else while she dealt with things nobody else would.

Often I would stumble in on her doing her homework in the early hours, memorising reports at the kitchen table or making a call from the car to check on a patient's progress. She let me see her working, but she didn't show it to anybody else.

Once we were at a restaurant with another couple from the hospital when she excused herself. She said she was going to the bathroom but she was making a call. When she returned to the table the others asked how it was going and Alice said, not so well. And then the conversation moved to something else – wine, the entrée, something like that – and everything was like it was before except for the shimmering blade of her fish knife. Her hands were trembling. 'Not so well' meant somebody had died. A woman, or maybe a child.

The point wasn't to ignore it. The point was to step back into the world of chatting about the weather and close the pocket diary containing pages of close handwriting listing fifty, sixty items a week: medication, appointments, human beings. The point was to be thorough and even and not make a mistake.

Alice was equally meticulous about what we consumed. As we rolled on the floor laughing she would line up the remaining pills in order of

7

chemical grouping. Once I moved a pill and, still laughing, her smile a little tighter, she took my hand and guided it back.

When she cupped a pill to my lips or withdrew the gleaming needle I would kiss her long, cool hands that touched sick and dying people every day. Because I knew what she went through I never asked why she liked to get fucked up. The real question was why she didn't do it more.

At nights we fell asleep watching small TV shows and in the mornings she would rail up and leave one for me on the bedside table while she had a shower. When she came out we'd fuck and kiss and she would dress for work and hold out her hand for the credit card while I ran the edge between my teeth.

We moved into a better building. We paid a decorator to fill it with new colours and furniture. We paid for restaurants, dry-cleaning, towaway zones, anything that broke. Things were rolling past. Nothing stuck.

We renewed our passports: single, no children. We kept it together. We kept us together.

We spent a long summer weekend in Sydney. We loaded up for the flight and were met at the airport by an old friend of hers who said hello and carried our bags and flipped down the glove-box door in the car park so we could take a hit before we'd even pulled out.

We spent four days not touching the food in expensive restaurants. We drank and wandered between clubs and hotel rooms and dumb tourist attractions, laughing. We sat in the National Gallery counting the colours in Aborigine paintings. That was our dreamtime. We were floating in millions of coloured dots.

Alice's friend gave us a farewell gift in the airport toilets. We drank Cointreau miniatures on the plane. We got home at nine a.m. I remember Alice wasn't on duty that morning. She climbed into the sheets and closed her eyes and started humming softly to herself, becoming lost in warm orange dreams. And then I got in the car and started driving down the motorway doing a hundred and forty-five.

I argued with her not to go. I thought we could fix it like we fixed everything else. I was wired into machines that kept me going. My busted bones started to knit. I thought we could pull it together if we just stuck it out but we couldn't. My healing was an anomaly. She could never go back.

She got a job working in a drug treatment centre in Sydney, up on the Cross. There was more heroin going into Australia than the whole of the United States. AIDS, hepatitis: there was plenty of work.

It took her one night to pack everything she would need. The rest she left for me: furniture, appliances, the record collection – everything. I didn't touch it. I never went back to that apartment. I guess the new tenants got it all. I didn't care. I couldn't deal with sorting it out. I was busy learning to walk. I left it like you'd leave a bad one-night stand. Nearly two years, gone. Like someone just snapped their fingers.

My body healed fast. I skipped the drink-driving charge because someone messed up the results at the laboratory. The results from blood samples taken at the hospital were excluded from the trial because they were covered by patient confidentiality, protected by the same doctors who blew the whistle on Alice. The judge deferred the sentence for dangerous driving because my injuries were bad. People were lining up to help. People felt sorry for me.

I lost the statistical work. My concentration had gone. Insurance covered me for a while. I found a place but I didn't like staying there. I had started having the nightmares: I didn't like being by myself.

The nightmares were the same sequence over and over: I'm lying in my bed and there's something in the hallway and I don't know what it is – it's just there, a shadow about the size of a man that absorbs all light at the entrance to my room. And I can't move. I know that if I challenge or attack it, it will leave, but I'm glued to the bed and I can't make any noise. So I start to struggle, and then shout. That's when I would wake up sweating, the sheets wet on the bed.

It got so bad I didn't want to sleep. The doctors wouldn't prescribe sedatives because of my medical history, so I started to drink to put myself out. That worked for a while. When it stopped working, I'd drink to keep myself awake. I started hitting the bars.

A bar was always open somewhere. I would sneak in when they opened for deliveries and perch alongside the parkies and trolley people. I even got to look like one of them.

If there was a pay phone around I'd use it sometimes to call her friends. They never knew where she was. I started going back to places we'd been together but she wasn't there. I even tried going back to the apartment, anxious now to see our possessions, but the new tenants wouldn't buzz me in. I must have looked a shock on the security monitor. I was haggard and wild-eyed, banging on the lens. That was a bad night. It might have done me good to see how things had changed, but who's to know – it might have made it worse.

I eventually settled down and became a regular at a little place called the Normandy on Pitt Street, just up from the old fire station. The front of the Normandy was a high brick wall with gold-coloured glass windows running along the top like arrow slots in a fort. The entrance was a black curtain with a chain draped across it and a sign that said Members Only. You signed in on a book at the door – as Smith, usually. The barman kept the shutters down during the day and turned off the lights at night. Out back was a card room where nobody played cards. You could slip back there and get anything you needed; do it, drop it and sit out at the bar.

In a strange way, it was a safe place for me. Heavy drinkers don't need to talk or cause trouble. There is a mutual agreement to just sit there and watch things slow down as you go numb, and nobody has anything to add, no commentary or footnote. If something was going down you looked away. People left me alone. I could think.

I couldn't remember the accident. All I recalled was the spin, and being cut out of the car. When I visited the wrecker's yard and saw the vehicle's remains I caught a glimmer of how close I had come but it vanished as quickly as I sensed it, like smoke. An accident doesn't stay in your mind. People say you never forget a thing like that but if it's really like that – really bad – you never remember.

The only memento I had was my right shoulder where I was thrown through the window and the glass crunched into the flesh. The scarring ran down the bicep almost to the elbow like pink milk turned sour. Now and then it would heat up and ache and a pustule would develop, and then a cube of glass would push through the skin: sharp, tiny proof.

And that's how things went. Before I realised it, I had settled into a nice little routine. I rebuilt my jazz collection. I scored some good shit with the insurance money. It's true I didn't get quite the same buzz off either of them now – I had to play everything louder and double the dose – but it started to work. It's difficult to count how many months it lasted exactly. My life had collapsed into a series of interiors with only glimpses of sunlight and streets in between.

II

Electric

Chapter 2

Raymond Beatty was six-one with a baby face and a goatee and asthma. He stuck out in the Normandy, but not too much. He was scratching the collar of his brand new polo-neck T and twirling his tiny cell phone in a circle on the bar with his index finger while he waited for a friend of his, a Mr Smith. We got talking while he waited. He was eight years younger than me and he had his own company, ITD. The initials didn't stand for anything. Raymond chose them from a survey that showed people judged them to be the three most reliable-sounding letters in the alphabet.

ITD's business was data retrieval: fixing systems that had been corrupted or failed. For instance, when a branch office's computers were caught in a fire or an angry employee tipped a coffee percolator into his machine, the company would pay Raymond to pull the data off the boxes and send it back. It sounded dull. It didn't sound difficult. I knew enough about binary languages to handle it. And nobody else was offering me work: I was down and out, no matter what I was pretending. So when he made his soft-faced offer of a job I accepted and spent the following night watching dry-cleaners try to steam the smell out of my old business shirts.

The company was on the sixth floor of a mirror-glass box in Newmarket, just out of the central city. The space was a maze of dividers. The only people who had offices with locking doors were Raymond and me. His looked out on the harbour across a desk made from a 120-pound Hawaiian redwood long-board. Mine was on the building's shady side looking out on the car park and a dance studio where schoolgirls got dropped off in utility vehicles by their rich, skinny mothers.

Every morning there was a new delivery of blackened casings waiting at reception, their high-tech guts stained with liquid or spilling out on the tiles. The receptionist, Holly, wrote stickers for each one with a pen she kept in a sensible holder around her neck. You went through the pile, picked up the one with your name on it and went to work.

The procedures were set. All I had to do was apply certain filters and applications, wait, and make copies of everything. If there were no results you took it to the next level, applying more complex algorithms, different software. There were many steps, and if they still didn't work you could send the hardware off to a lab where they would put the disk under an electron microscope to scan the magnetic surface, reading off the zeros and ones of the binary code like thumbprints. It could all be retrieved. Phone numbers, shopping purchases, love letters, tax statements, insurance, magazine subscriptions, credit card numbers, pornography: the information never goes away.

Not that it stopped people trying. We had one guy who carefully unplugged his machine and took it outside and drove a delivery van over it twice. We had someone shit in the box. There was discussion about whether they did it on the desk in the office or took it into a rest room to use one of the stalls.

A woman threw hers out of a fourth-storey window on to a cement sidewalk, which we all acknowledged was pretty impressive. It takes a good, strong arm to lug a metal computer casing not only through the glass but out far enough so it clears the structure all the way down.

Most of the damage took place during a tax month. Workers would trash their machines to claim insurance. Employers tried to delete records and files so auditors couldn't use them. A sales manager who was behind on targets sent a power spike through a network to fry every machine that was connected. But the majority of events were just spontaneous: someone losing it or whatever.

We pulled dead goldfish and oxygen weed out of the slots. We found pools of soda and milk shakes: meat pies, toothpaste. Boxes that were stomped on and pummelled with a bat. And a lot of fires. Once I cracked open the shell and found the wires still burning inside.

There is a lot of rage in the workplace directed against machines. There was always the joke going around that you hurt the ones you love, so what was wrong with these people? Didn't they have families to take it out on? Pets? They didn't even have friends. All they had was this pathetic beige box.

The staff at the firm were mostly guys who were the age when jokes like that seemed funny. They had been earning good money since they dropped out of school. They didn't want anything that couldn't be bought. They were twenty years old and hadn't made any mistakes yet, and until they did the world's imperfections and other people's mistakes would remain a mystery to them: an object of fun.

ITD also did security jobs where we were paid to trawl through a system and see what we could find. It was a strict rule that only Raymond met the owners of the information. We wouldn't have recognised any of them in the street. But going through the data you got to know a lot about each person's life. You started to sense who they were.

After the data was revived and before I wrote out the report I would spend some quiet time looking for a clue as to whatever had brought these people to boiling point. This wasn't part of the job. I just did it. And I never found anything directly. There might be a letter of resignation that stopped before it had been finished or a note breaking off a relationship. There was porn, the same images duplicated and passed around until they stopped meaning anything, like a word repeated over and over. No threats or treatises – just folders of business letters and accounts and memos, bland office small talk in triplicate; something one of their kids had scribbled. These people were normal, and that was pretty much all you needed to know.

I kept looking through it regardless, even if it meant missing a deadline. I didn't mind doing overtime – in fact, I was disappointed when I was finished because I didn't want to go home. So I'd head back up to the Normandy and drink, and when I'd had a skinful, I'd go out driving. It cleared my head. At two in the morning the streets were empty and straight and perfectly lit. I liked seeing how fast I could take the corners – full pedal, no seat belt, the music up loud. Faster and faster.

For the office Christmas party Raymond hired an army shooting range out by the Desert Road, in the flatlands where the mountain air blew cold across the red earth. In the middle of the plain was a row of TV sets and old scooters and assorted white goods and we got to blast the shit out of it all with hired semi-automatic handguns. The army provided us with earmuffs and protective eyewear and fifty free rounds. They showed us how to load the clip and aim and fire two-handed, like in the movies.

The noise was frightening at first but we got used to it and the recoil, and soon the gunfire was richocheting across the dunes. We were missing targets as large as a washing machine because our tears were fogging up the yellow goggles. Even the army instructors supervising the ordnance- and weapon-handling were laughing so hard they had to sit down. It just kept getting funnier, watching this metal box or that tuned mechanism pop and skip between the clumps of whip-grass like it was trying to escape, and the smoke had a sweet smell, like charcoal.

After all the jokes about people snapping at the office, here we were attacking other people's hard work and laughing as it came apart. There was no irony in that. It was always going to come apart. The question wasn't if. It was just a matter of when, and how.

I still wasn't sleeping. In the mornings I lay in bed watching the sun rise until the room was bright. When I got up I shook breakfast out of a sachet and did a line so I could stay calm and jam on the way to work.

The ITD car park always smelled of oil and exhaust fumes and cigarettes, and as you walked through it you could hear the little girls stomping upstairs, jumping up and down like they were dancing on the spot.

I swiped my card and stepped into the marble foyer where the ceiling tubes burned 24/7. I said hi to Holly, got a soda from the kitchen, picked up my allotted box and wheeled it into my office and kicked the door shut with my foot. I didn't drink the soda right away: I just rolled the cold can across my forehead. The idea was to get as much done as I could before the slump hit because even though I wasn't sleeping, I still got pretty tired. When the slump did hit there was nothing to do but get out the bottle of vodka I kept in the bottom drawer and top up the soda with it and maybe do some quick chop on the little camping mirror I kept handy for the mornings.

It was always the same. The job I was working on that day was like any other. The damage to the machine wasn't malicious: there was water and salt in the system – sea salt, it turned out, blown in from the west coast although I couldn't tell by looking. I found that out much later on.

I cracked the case and hooked up the drive and started the repair systems and looked at the screen and, as it unfolded, suddenly saw this wonderful thing.

I doubt it would have looked wonderful to anyone else. They might have understood it. They might have been able to make more with it – my physics is not that strong – but I doubt it would have meant as much to them as it did to me at that point in time. It was a single formula that I recognised. I understood what it described and I felt it, right down the back of my neck.

I scrolled down.

F/o/ 586

$$c = \sqrt{gh}$$

Velocity structure in a long wave. C is wave speed. H is water depth. G is gravity. Shallow waves are non-dispersive. The wave speed depends on the water depth.

$$\frac{L}{\sqrt{gh}}$$

Reflection of a wave in a closed basin. The length of the basin is L, the depth h. The wave is reflected at the wall of the basin.

All the calculations were based on the mathematics of waves. They described wave speed and depth, how high they would rise before they fell. The clearness of the swell, gathering strength, building, reaching up to the sky and then breaking. Falling into white foam.

Crashing.

The machinery in the box purred, ticking its way through the zeros and ones, reconstituting the formulae. Rebuilding the sea.

Scientists used to think that turbulence was an engineering problem, but really it's about chaos. The flow of fluid is a symptom of the disorder that exists in the universe on every scale. Chaos says things in the universe change suddenly because time and possibilities are infinite, a four-dimensional space. We move through it like a blade moving through water: our reality is the part of time and space that clings to the blade.

Inevitably, this boundary layer of reality breaks up. It tears away and takes us with it, like a wave. We go from calm, we build up and crash through to calm again.

Chaos theory says this will happen. All it takes is the movement of a single atom. A single decision and you're alive or dead. Reality is in constant motion.

I spent the whole morning going through everything in the box. I found beautiful spirals and curves,
blue shapes pulsing against fine turquoise grids.
Green and grey demarcations of basins unfolded like
origami. Yellow peaks broke against troughs of
black. Perfect numbers, silent and clear. It was like
seeing a storm from far above: it was calm, and it was
cool and it was sweet.

I couldn't take my eyes off it.

Chapter 3

I found the job number in Holly's files while she was out to lunch and traced the client address. I wrote a delivery slip to make it look like the box had been sent on a courier and then carried it out to my car and drove it across town through the traffic and the glare.

That summer was turning into one of the hottest on record. All the tenants in my building were leaving their air-conditioning running around the clock. If you put your hand on the wall you could feel the heat from the units blasting away on the other side. One burned out in the apartment below me and almost started a fire. The corridors smelled like wax.

People were getting scratchy in the heat. You could hear arguments and strange voices rising up through the floors: doors slamming, the TV running at odd hours. The local gas station kept selling out of ice. People were buying it to put in the bath. There were a lot of parties. There was music everywhere, and talk about global warming and the vanishing coastline and how the hole in the ozone layer was getting bigger. The hole had been made by the countries at the top of the world but we were the ones getting burned.

The address was on the edge of Albert Park in a building that was one of the oldest in the city. It stood twelve storeys high with a walled courtyard and vines climbing the grey stone like the wrinkles of a brain. City real estate had got expensive since the eighties and a place like this was real hard to get. There were only a small number of apartments in the building and tenants always took care to pass on the leases to friends and associates. You had to know the right people.

The flat was right up top. I pressed the intercom and said I was delivering the computer. A man buzzed me in. I walked into the octagonal foyer and took the old gated elevator to the top. The lift shaft was cool in the heat.

The guy who opened the door was about my age. He was wearing black suit pants and a singlet. His bare feet were bony and pale. He was unshaven with a long face and grey hair cropped close and his eyes were black saucers. I checked the slip.

'Jules Way?'

He waved me in with his cigarette. He was wearing two watches on his left wrist.

I followed him into the lounge. The room was dark because the curtains were half drawn, blue sky and the park peeking through the gap. I put the box down on the floor by the phone. The answering-machine light was blinking. The bookcases were lined with photographs and loose change and snow-shaker paperweights: Cairo, Christmas Island, Cayenne. An old reel-to-reel Revox tape player was running on the bottom shelf, pushing Miles in Japan through German speakers.

'You like jazz?' I said.

'Used to be my dad's. I know nothing about it.'

In the centre of the room was a set of dark red chairs and a black lacquered coffee table. The table was cluttered with bottles and cigarette packets and a long piece of foil unfolded on a copy of *Scientific American*. A credit card had been used to cut two long lines of powder on the wood. Jules looked at me looking at it and smiled.

'Want a hit?' he said.

I slipped out something of my own.

'Fucking excellent,' he said.

He set it all out. We pushed the chairs apart and sat on the floor.

'Start with this,' he said. 'Then this.'

The tape sounded good. I shaded my eyes with my hand. Everything kicked in at once. The music became perfect and clear. The single strip of light that fell between the curtains caught the dust in the air and held it there, making it dance.

'That's some deck,' I said.

'He took good care of it.'

'Was he a musician?'

Jules shook his head. 'He was a Queen's Messenger at the embassy in Paris.'

'That's where you grew up?'

Jules nodded. 'Hated it. My French was bad. I never really learned. I could talk about everyday things and read but I couldn't keep up with the conversation if people spoke quickly. And then my mother died, and my father brought me back. We had a black Citroën. The movers packed the car in a shipping container, packed everything in around it. Like a big present.'

'Have you still got the car?'

'My father drove it off the Kapiti Coast. Killed himself. Left-hand drive. He'd been drinking and he was on the wrong side of the road.'

I pushed up my sleeve.

'Shit,' he said. 'Good one.'

'Southern motorway. Goes all the way up.'

'I went back overseas. I said I was going to finish my degree but really I was going back to whatever I had then.'

'You're a mathematician, right?'

He nodded, looking slightly puzzled.

'Yes. I'm glad I came back,' he said. 'If I'd stayed in France and become a citizen I would have been eligible for the draft. Mathematicians make terrible soldiers, did you know that?'

'I didn't.'

'I mean, not all of them. Yule was an army statistician in World War I. Girard – trigonometry – was an engineer in the Dutch army.' Jules sniffed, wiping the white rim around his nose. 'But Burch- nall – differential operators – lost a leg in Belgium.

Dandelin – intersection of a cone – ended up fighting Napoleon. Konrad Knopp – generalised limits - was wounded as an officer. Gaston Julia – rational functions – had his face shot off. Teichmüller – geometry – killed. Möbius dodged the Prussian draft. He threatened to stab anyone who tried to force him to fight. An appropriate tautology.' He chopped out another line. 'You have that.'

'Thanks.'

'Mathematics delivers and detonates every projectile,' he said. 'The history of our vocation is run through with a sword. You can't get away from that. It's part of what I do. Mankind loves explosions. Ever since discovering ballistics we've fashioned our theories after its mechanics. We want things to explode into being, to accelerate and slow down like a shell. We want to puncture objects. The magic bullet, the silver bullet – that's all people talk about, you notice? Why do they love bullets and shells?'

'Because it's so much fucking fun,' I said.

'Have you fired a gun?'

I told him about the party we had at work. 'Handguns and a semi-automatic rifle, an A-1 or M-1 – something like that.'

He laughed. 'Superb. And you shot what?'

'TVs, washing machines. And it felt great, shooting all that stuff up. I thought bullets only made holes but if you hit something at the right angle it literally jumps and explodes, like it's released.'

'I think the race to develop the atomic bomb was the last great romance of the twentieth century,' he

28

said. 'We're living in the world those men invented. We're at its mercy because they were hard-working geniuses who thought of it first. Men standing in the Nevada heat measuring the Holy Grail with slide rules. We are figments of their imagination: ants on their kitchen bench.'

Jules picked up a pack of cigarettes and shook one out. He waved the unlit cigarette in his right hand, using his left to straighten the matchbook on the magazine cover.

'The point of science is to describe the world,' he said. 'By advancing theories we construct it anew. Science is ego: I describe what it is, and then it becomes that way. How is your world shaped? It's shaped by other people's minds. All these different theories fighting it out. How the universe began. What light's made of. And all we can do is wait to see which one is right: to find out who's dreaming, and who's awake.'

Again he tapped the line on the table.

'Although as realities go, I believe this is the finest available. Don't you think? The Jules Way line theory.'

'Let's test it,' I said.

'I'm mixing it with another.'

'Fast or slow theory?'

We did some more and lay back and let it and the music wash over us both.

Down in the park tourists were waiting to photograph each other in front of the fountain, lining up in the heat. The trees muffled the city noise and the chemicals kept us talking.

In Chicago, scientists generated a series of random numbers between one and a hundred using atomic decay, then asked volunteers to visualise numbers above fifty before viewing them. The results were all above fifty. The volunteers had changed them with a thought.

In Los Alamos, scientists made a beryllium atom appear in two places at once. They duplicated quantum superpositions by making the same object appear in two different places, two different universes.

In Auckland, Sam Usher and Jules Way pressed the bare soles of their feet against the edge of a black table dusted with white powder while a guitarist from twenty years ago played the same funk riff over and over until the tape ran off the spool, the lick of ribbon whipping lazily across the heads.

'I'm glad I met you, Sam. Not a lot of people get this stuff – not in Auckland, anyway.'

'You must enjoy the coast. For your work.'

He looked puzzled again.

'The waves,' I said. 'The turbulence theory.'

He blinked and nodded, finally working it out. 'You're talking about the work on the computer? It's not mine. It's my girlfriend's.'

He took a photograph down from the bookcase. She was blonde and pretty.

'Candice Strange. She prefers it if people call her Candy.'

'That stuff was amazing. There was something about it.' I scratched my shoulder. 'Just something – I don't know.'

Jules was still looking at the photograph.

'She could get a good job with the right people if she wanted. But she doesn't. So she's doing nothing instead, and I'm stuck at the university. And here we are. Contending with this city.'

'You need to travel.'

'Maybe. It's not that bad. Auckland's like a dog that isn't too smart. It can be fun. We should get together and have some fun, Sam.'

I said I'd like that.

Chapter 4

We arranged to meet late at night after the temperature had dropped. I pulled together enough stuff to make myself worth talking to and turned up at the party his friends were having at a place on the slope of Mount Eden. The house stuck out from the volcanic cone like a diving board. The hosts had either lost themselves in the crowd or maybe fallen into the valley. There were as many guests inside the house as outside, all stumbling around the furniture and the neighbouring gardens. Tired kids lay around smoking barefoot in the hall. When I came in they looked up like I was another passenger joining the queue. Good times departed regularly from the different rooms.

I felt blocked up and antsy. I ducked into the bathroom and pulled a beer out of the tub and went looking for Jules and the woman he had his arm around in the photograph.

I recognised Candy when I saw her. She was standing at the end of the hallway stroking the moons of her fingernails. She was as tall as she had looked in the photographs except she was in colour now: straight blonde hair and a red silk dress with slit arms and a buttoned collar.

She shifted, but not in reaction to my approach. There was sweat on her round cheeks. Her pupils were stretched black and wide. She was rubbing one foot against the other. Her toenails were painted red.

Up close, her hair looked darker beneath the blonde. She was stroking a strand of it behind her ears. There was a round inoculation scar on her left shoulder. I leaned next to her so I could look at it and her throat. I wanted to see the pulse in her neck where the blood was jumping in the vein. She was rolling her jaw and chewing but there was nothing in her mouth.

She looked at me.

'What are you looking at?' she said.

I introduced myself and she smiled but she hadn't really heard.

'I'm Candice,' she said. 'My friends call me Candy.'

'You don't look like a Candice,' I said. 'With the kimono.'

'It's a cheongsam. It's Chinese, not Japanese.'

'I'm a friend of Jules,' I said again.

She tugged absently at the stud in her ear, still not listening. We stood in the hall for a good long time thinking a lot of things but not saying much.

Much later I followed her outside to the back porch where Jules was looking out over the city. He was wearing the suit jacket with the trousers now, over an old surfing T-shirt. Candy leaned on the rail and put her arm around him. She kissed him, faintly. He smiled but didn't look at her. She wiped her nose, pushing it upwards with the palm of her free hand and sniffing, wiping her face.

I blinked. I tracked the lights of the houses as they stretched along the hills. The city was spread out below us like coins in a pool.

'All these people,' Jules said. 'I guess they're watching TV. Do you watch a lot of TV, Sam?'

'Yes. Do you?'

'Of course. Some people don't, though.'

Candy folded her arms. 'It's cold out here.'

'Didn't you have a jacket?' Jules said.

'I think it's in one of the rooms.'

'Do you want me to get it?'

'It'll be okay.'

'You have to be careful.'

'I'll be fine.' She bent down and picked up a bottle. 'Do you like Jagermeister, Sam?' she said.

'I don't drink it often.'

'It's nice. Try some.'

'Thank you.'

I drank some and handed it back.

'You don't like it, do you?' she said.

'It's fine.'

'But you do like it?' She smiled. 'You don't.'

'It's a terrible drink,' Jules said. 'You have a whole universe of drinks to choose from and you drink that.'

She put her arm back around him. 'You're in a lovely mood tonight, darling,' she said.

He shrugged.

'Jules is grumpy,' she said. She was laughing. She kissed his neck.

'Don't let her make you drink any more of that crap, Sam. She's been going round offering it to total strangers and fucking up their evening.'

'It's fine once,' she said.

'What isn't?'

She pulled him closer. 'He's unharmed,' she said. 'Are you here with anyone?' she asked me.

'Jesus,' he said.

'I'm only asking him.'

'No,' I said.

Candy twisted to look back at the hills.

'It's so pretty,' she said. 'It looks so far away. It makes you want to go closer.'

'We should go somewhere,' I said.

'Let's go to the sugar factory.'

'I couldn't handle it,' Jules said.

'You don't have to handle it. You just have to come along. Do you want to go to the sugar factory, Sam?'

'That'd be cool,' I said.

They had a black Mercedes. Candy drove while Jules slouched in the passenger seat and I stretched out in the back.

The sugar factory was the old sugar refinery at the mouth of the Waitemata Harbour. The loading wharf was just east of a point called Needle's Eye. I grew up around there – all the kids used to go swimming off the wharf. We'd creep into the

35

grounds at midnight and run behind the trees and jump off screaming and yelling.

Candy's hands were steady on the wheel. We drove past the bars and the park and the marina. We crossed the harbour bridge and she pulled off the motorway, the city sparkling behind us before it disappeared.

She drove fast under the bridge, the tyres squealing on the old, narrow roads. The people who had bought houses here dwelled in the shade of the oldest money in Auckland. Restored villas slept behind venetian blinds and hedges trimmed by hired gardeners. In the back seat, I sat up. Just driving through here had brought back the odour of comfortable living, like perfume. Candy watched me in the rear-view mirror. Her eyes smiled.

Green grass feathered the cement seals and pelicans. The sun warmed the schoolyard bitumen. I was remembering lunchtime fights and theatre groups in the assembly hall – teenage actors flipping signs around their necks that showed a magic spell. Forest. Invisible.

We were coming up to the gates of the sugar factory. Candy cut the lights and dropped into neutral and let us coast down the hill, the way paved by moonlight. As we approached the water the big shapes of the refinery buildings rose up, silhouetted by stars. A single security light brushed the waves white.

Candy tapped the brakes and pulled off the driveway into the cover of the trees. The car's heavy suspension bounced on the hardened lawn. She brought it gently to a stop and killed the engine.

'Where the fuck are we?' Jules said.

'The water looks beautiful,' Candy said. 'Let's go swimming.'

Jules laughed. He took the bottle of Jagermeister out of the glove box and unscrewed the cap.

'Come on,' she said. 'It's night.'

'Sharks feed at night.'

'There are no sharks in the harbour.'

'The shark to be scared of is the shark you can't see.'

She rolled her eyes. 'Give me your shirt.'

'Just go like that.'

'Give it to me. Are you coming, Sam?'

'Sure thing.'

We struggled to undress in the car. I pulled off my shoes and my watch and my jacket and balled them up in the back seat. Candy twisted out of her Chinese dress, her shins banging the dashboard. Jules took off his T-shirt and gave it to her and put his jacket back on over his bare chest. As she put the shirt on she knocked the steering wheel and the horn sounded. We froze. Nothing happened. The place was dead. Jules pushed his seat back and closed his eyes.

Candy and I stepped out. The air outside was warm. A low fence cut with names and insults ran by the trees. We felt our way along it, found the gap in the scrub and disappeared.

For a minute, we couldn't see anything. She held

my hand while I felt with my feet for the steps cut into the clay that led down to the wharf. We could taste the salt in the air. We were too warm to feel the branches scratching our skin. The night shadow of the refinery buildings and the wharf rose up from the rocks and white surf.

We stepped on to the wharf. Waves smacked against the poles. Wet seaweed floated like a dirty wig in the water. Candy steadied herself to look down. I didn't understand why she had bothered with the T-shirt. She had wrapped it tight around her torso but she wasn't trying to cover her cunt.

I dropped her hand and jumped. When I hit, the cold rush pushed the air out of my lungs and the thoughts out of my head. Brightness flashed and the water closed over me and then I was walking gently through nothing and my skin turned warm again. I was tumbling. A wave rolled me against the seaweed. As I turned upside down the salt water ran into my nose and down the back of my throat and I coughed and sucked it in.

It was dark. I couldn't tell where the surface was. I stretched out my arms. My head was still spinning. I started to cough. I felt for the rocks but lost them and another wave rolled back and pushed me through the seaweed. When I opened my eyes I saw nothing, up or down. Blackness and silence. And then my ears started to ring.

The seconds were turning slow and lazy. My body was becoming numb. I was fully awake to it. Everything went black. Everything went light. I tried to slow it down, opening my eyes. I saw white traces. A big swell came in and lifted me. I broke surface and retched, opening my eyes at the exact moment Candy jumped, her body catching the moonlight for a second before the black water swallowed her.

The inlet wasn't wide. The distance to the land's edge was only a few strokes. There was raw metal alongside, the rusting remains of a boat ramp – I was remembering all this now as the drugs and alcohol spun my head. I treaded water, waiting for the dizziness to pass.

Candy came up.

'Isn't it cool?' she shouted. 'Isn't this the coolest fucking thing?'

My ears had blocked. She dog-paddled over to me, laughing and coughing at the same time. She put her arms around my neck, keeping us a short distance apart. We were both gasping. My chest was tight and my vision was spotting. Her touch was warmer than the water but as cold as my skin. She ran her hand down my shoulder, testing the touch of my scars.

'You got cut,' she said.

The breeze was louder. Waves hit the uprights of the wharf and broke and hushed. I was shaking. The glass in my shoulder ached. I could hardly see her face in the moonlight. She tracked the scars down to my elbow. Another swell came in and pushed her close.

As she got out of the water I thought I saw

something on the skin of her back. She pulled her shirt down to cover it before I could tell what it was. She climbed up on the rocks. I followed her out.

Jules was still leaning back in the front seat of the Mercedes, the bottle balanced on his chest. He wound down the window and handed her the Jagermeister and she drank some and passed me the bottle. I could taste her spit and lipstick.

We did what we could to dry ourselves. Candy squeezed back into her Chinese dress, the silk turning black between her shoulders. When I put my shirt on it stuck to my stomach.

Jules was waking up now, looking at us both and talking more. I was trying to figure out the vibe between them. People with tired faces have always interested me. If someone looks pretty and calm you start the conversation with small talk, but if they have shadows under their eyes you know what matters to them straight away. Jules and Candy seemed preoccupied, like this was a break in their schedule. It made me wonder what they weren't talking about. I put it down to paranoia and the spots that were jumping around everything I looked at. I put it away for now.

We shivered on the drive back. The radio was playing and the heater was on. The sugar factory was black on the water. We started to sharpen up.

Candy shifted gears as we came to the bridge. Jules wound down the sun roof to watch the planets as we drove past. I leaned between the seats to change the music. My arm brushed hers. She glanced at me in the rear-view mirror again and said nothing.

Chapter 5

His father's legacy meant Jules was still invited to consulate receptions. Jules said they were no big deal: just a really good party filled with people you wouldn't meet anywhere else. That sounded like a good deal to me but he kept apologising for it as if it would be a bore to attend.

'I think you'll enjoy it, Sam,' he said.

'I don't want to be tagging along.'

'You're not tagging along. You're with us.'

We got a taxi down to the waterfront. The long streets behind Princes Wharf were marked for development but progress had stalled. A council crew was digging a trench under the road, chiselling a track in the shit-yellow clay, but the shop fronts remained boarded and padlocked, waiting to be demolished by better men.

The consulate was down a side-street, a small white building with red-eyed security cameras hanging above the door and a six-foot iron gate softened by years of grey paint. Jules pressed the intercom and the gate swung open.

A security guard met us at the steps while an official in a waistcoat checked the invitation. He shook Jules' hand and gave us name tags and showed us into what he called the Blue Room, which was in fact green with a high, decorated white plaster ceiling and old green and gold furniture being tripped over by about a hundred people. A three-piece band were playing cover versions in the far corner, their PA drowned out by the noise of the conversation. People were shouting indiscriminately, safe behind their different languages.

Velvet drapes were drawn across the windows and the room was heavy with cigarette smoke. Waiters in aprons and black tie were rushing to serve champagne and beer on wide silver trays. The bar staff were pulling wet bottles from bins stacked under the serving tables, spilling ice and water that shone on the floor like polished stones.

The crowd was thick with the expressions and gestures of people who had known each other for years. I didn't recognise anyone or understand what any of them were saying.

I turned to speak to Candy but she'd gone. A man in a white suit came over and extended his hand to greet me in another language I didn't know. I shook it and smiled and shrugged. His name tag said 'Dedit'. He waited, and then Jules cut in and replied for me. I don't know what he said but the man's face brightened. He patted my shoulder before moving on.

'He's an old friend,' Jules said.

'I didn't get what he said.'

'It's kind of hard to hear.'

The band had turned up their PA now.

'Where's he from?' I shouted.

'You're never sure with these guys. Diplomats are surrounded by this little force field. My dad had one. When I was born the delivery was in Paris but technically I was here all the time, in New Zealand. They carry their countries around with them wherever they go.'

He turned to speak to someone else. I looked around. The clothes and décor said nothing had changed in this place since 1965. Whichever country we were supposed to be standing in, time hadn't moved either.

I saw Candy through the crowd. She was going upstairs. I followed, peeling off my name tag and dropping it on the carpeted staircase. She was headed to the rest room. I followed her in.

The handbasins shone. Someone had dropped a glass on the floor, crunching shards between the black and white tiles. The two women at the mirror were unalarmed. Some guy following his girlfriend: it looked like innocent fun. I smiled and said how's it going and they turned back to each other.

I figured Candy would take the end cubicle so she wouldn't have people listening on either side. I rapped on the door twice, fast, and whispered.

'It's me, Sam,' I said.

She opened up and I pushed inside and she latched the door. We listened to the two women finish and stumble out of the rest room, giggling. Candy smiled and leaned back. I stood up. She took the baggie out of her purse and dumped a good third across the top of the cistern.

Someone else came in and went into a cubicle. We weren't panicking. The more people making noise, the better.

She resealed the baggie. I gave her my card. She made a line of powder and cut it with three diagonal strokes, tapping the dividing edge and running the card along her tongue, the pink conclusion to the ceremony. I rolled a bill. Outside someone ran a tap. I heard a man laugh.

When I was finished she took the bill and held her hair back as she bent over the cistern. And then we stood there sniffing while she took out a compact and checked her make-up. I looked at her and smiled and she started to giggle.

'Don't.' She held her nose. 'You're making mc laugh.'

I dipped my little finger in the baggie.

'One for the road.'

I held it out. She took it lightly in her lips and rolled her tongue around the tip and the nail. She clicked the compact shut.

'Let's go,' she said.

When we walked back into the room we were together on the same level, in the same place, seeing and hearing the same colours and sounds. We made our way to the windows, stepping over the puddles and cigarette stubs. I pushed the drapes aside so we could sit on the sill and stopped. There was no glass in the frame, only black painted plaster. All the windows in the room were false.

Candy lit up on the sill while I got us some champagne. As I stepped close to hand her the glass she looked away and let her shoulder brush my leg. I put my weight on it and she braced against me a little harder. I made a joke about the dancing but she didn't laugh. We were both idling, waiting for something to happen.

Jules was talking to the guy in the white suit again, waving his hands.

'Jules looks like it's his high school reunion,' I said.

'It practically is,' Candy said. 'He's known these people since he was a kid.'

'Do you go to many things like this?'

She nodded. 'When we first met, in New York. I'd graduated and was waiting tables and he was running an experiment to see how fast he could spend his inheritance. He was hanging out with his dad's old crowd: embassy, civil service people – you know the sort of thing. It was better than sitting in a café all winter.'

'You do a lot of travelling.'

'We used to. We had a lot of money back then.'

'But not now.'

'Well, Jesus – you know the lifestyle. It doesn't last long.' She stirred her champagne and watched the bubbles stick to her finger. 'That crowd is so far from practical things. Half the time I'd jet lag and forget getting off the plane and wake up in the taxi

and ask the driver what city it was. And Jules was just
as bad. We'd hook up with someone and party with
them until it was time to be driven back to the
airport. Once we forgot to take our luggage with us.
There were years of this. I couldn't hear myself
think. And then, like you say, we ran out of money.'

'Bad debts,' I said.

'Yeah.' She nodded, looking at me. 'Very bad
debts. We figured things here would be safe. Jules'
dad had left him the apartment so we came back and
kicked the tenants out, moved our stuff in.'

'And now you're here.'

'Yeah.' She squinted. 'But you know what? All
the excitement got boring. The cities and airports
and parties in a second language – you get bored just
being the girlfriend. We stopped talking because
there was nothing about ourselves we wanted to talk
about. I mean: we'd be there in some fantastic
fucking place going blah, blah.' She twirled her
cigarette in the air. 'You can't escape yourself, right?
I had work to get on with.'

'I was interested in that.'

'Jules said.' She smiled. 'You know about fluid
dynamics?'

'I've read about it.'

'When a blade passes through liquid,' she said, 'a
thin boundary layer of the fluid sticks to it.
Eventually this layer is torn off the blade by the
liquid that isn't moving, and this tearing covers the
surface of the blade with eddies and vortexes. On a

47

microscopic scale, the blade is stalled by this turbulence. It stops, then starts, stops and starts again –
millions of times a second. The vibrations shake the
blade apart.

'If you can design a blade that decreases this
turbulence – this fluid flow – by even an increment,
you create a more efficient impeller or turbine. And
if the design was truly efficient, you could change
the world. Ships and planes could travel further on
less fuel. You could irrigate deserts and generate
power from the tide and reduce fossil fuel emissions.
You could shift the world economy with a single
blade.'

'Sounds simple.'

'Well, it's what I'm trying to do,' she said. 'And it
is simple. A turbine creates order out of chaos: it's
about grace and symmetry and flow, like this
graceful machine. And I think the shape of the blade
will be seductive, like a body. Like the curve of a
girl's shoulder. Like Marie Antoinette's breast
moulding the first champagne flute.'

'How do you know that?'

'Woman's intuition.' She smiled. 'And a supercomputer. You test them in virtual space.'

'Now it sounds complicated.'

'I don't care. It's my heat-sink. I have anxiety and
fear and I pour it into this. My blade redirects it.
What do you have?'

My glass was empty.

'I guess I just snoop around,' I said. 'Put things
together.'

'But that's your job, right? Digging up the past.'

'It's not quite as romantic as that. It's pretty dry, actually. People's files, their work.'

'What sort of work?'

I shrugged. 'Letters.'

'You know,' she said.

'All right. Love letters to the secretary. Bondage photos. Entire tax years. Scatological pictures in folders named "budget". Things people put away and don't think you'll ever find.'

'Have you ever found anything really bad?' she said.

'Like what?'

'Like children.'

'Not yet.'

'What would you do if you did?'

'Legally, I can't do anything.'

'But if you did.'

'I'd probably wipe it, or tell the right people about it. There are a lot of ways you can make sure something like that is dealt with.'

'So you'd draw the line somewhere.'

'I think everyone does.'

'I think you like your job,' Candy said. 'I think you get a kick out it.'

'You know what?' I said. 'It reassures me, putting this stuff together. So many things in my life just fly apart.'

When I said it, I realised how much I meant it. Everything breaks up. Everything ends. Things get worse and worse until they break like an old ceiling heavy with rainwater.

'That's what you think?' Candy said.

'That's how it feels.'

'Turbulence,' she said.

We didn't want to come down. We did another line, in the men's room. I lit her cigarettes and talked about modal jazz, why the band wasn't very good. She talked about karma and neutrinos, the particles passing through matter every second: through walls, metal, food, skin. How scientists built strange receivers to catch them, lowering vacuum tubes into giant tanks deep underground, waiting months in a potash mine for the flash of Cherenkov radiation to illuminate the darkness of what they guessed was there but couldn't prove.

On the way back in the taxi Jules put his arm around my shoulder.

'So did you have a good time, Sam?' he said. 'Did you meet anyone nice?'

I said something – I can't remember what. Candy kept staring out the window like she was alone in the car.

Chapter 6

The first power cut hit at eight-thirty in the morning. The company supplying the central business district called it an outage but it really was a cut: a contractor laying pipe drove a digger blade through one of the four cables feeding power into the lower half of the city.

Everything along Hobson and Quay Streets went dead. The residents and office workers had to stand around scratching their heads for an hour while the power was re-routed along a second line. When it came back on there was no announcement: the first thing anyone knew about it was a power spike surging through the lines. Every computer that was still plugged in had its brains blown out.

By nine the phones at ITD were ringing off the hook. Raymond was calling everyone on their mobiles and telling them to get in fast. I got the call and said okay and then took a shower and shaved and made some coffee and drank it slowly, staring out the window. I wasn't rushing for anybody.

The stack of boxes in reception was bigger than usual. When I arrived I grabbed two off the top and wheeled them into my office. Taped to my monitor was a message from Raymond that said Where Are

You?!? I left it there while I got to work. If something I needed to read appeared on the screen under the note, I scrolled around it.

Holly came in and asked why I'd put that box on the courier the other day, and where was the receipt? I waved her away, saying I was too busy. She couldn't argue with that. Everything in the last twenty-four hours had been rendered irrelevant by the fate of countless billion zeros and ones that needed to be unpicked like so much hemp and sold back to the people who'd typed them up in the first place. People with ties and mobiles, business diaries, information. Documents, memos, minutes, notices: on and on and on. The machines clicked and whirred, putting it all back together brick by brick.

I thought about what Candy had said: about how I liked snooping around. Raymond's note fluttered in the current from the air-conditioning: Where Are You?!?

I picked up the phone and called the university.

The semester didn't start for months but Jules was scheduled to give a series of orientation lectures for foreign-language students that week. The lectures were an introduction to the physics course: a primer for students who were qualified in physics and maths but not English. I picked an afternoon session. With most of the students still on holiday the university looked demobilised.

The auditorium was old with a sloping floor and a line of three blackboards at the front. The students filed in five minutes early, the girls laughing behind their hands and the boys showing off. They looked clear-faced and adolescent. I hid behind them at the back of the room.

The kids sat up straight when Jules entered but he ignored them. He didn't introduce himself or announce the topic. He dropped his books on the lectern and turned to the first blackboard and started writing. A respectful buzz ran through the room. Clearly this was how lectures went in this country.

As he chalked up numbers, white dust settled on the blackboard sill. A few of the students talked among themselves. A few sat patiently and waited for him to finish what he was writing.

He didn't. By the time Jules had filled the first board and moved to the second, the students worked out that it was their job to keep up with the stubby chalk numerals and parentheses and the yards of English that accompanied it whether they understood or not. They struggled to copy words they couldn't read. Many were still on the second blackboard when Jules had finished the third.

They were expecting him to stop and summarise, but he didn't. Instead he went back and started again on the first board without wiping it clean, then the second. He kept writing until the dark green paint became light grey, then almost white. He started to write faster and faster, ignoring the sighs and murmurs, the growing sounds of confusion.

The students didn't complain outright. They probably didn't know how to, in English. As he built up the palimpsest, the chalk writing began to disintegrate: words on words, numbers on numbers.

At the end of the hour he was still writing. First the bolder pupils closed their books and tiptoed from the room. The others followed. And then the whole auditorium had emptied and I was alone in the back row watching Jules scratching on the boards, his words turning to dust in the afternoon sun.

I walked him to his apartment afterwards. He spooned four sugars into his coffee and laughed at my question.

'Of course they'll complain,' he said. 'They complain all the time. It doesn't matter. People used to be inspired to think, to change things, but not any more. Universities are outmoded. The thinking taught in these places is redundant. Academics won't admit that their time has passed, but it has. Corporations do the thinking now, and the military. That's where the real research is done. Everything else is navel-gazing.

'People don't realise how they're being left behind and they don't care. They won't fight for it. And because of that, the universities will be gone. They'll wither and die. We'll import knowledge from other countries and corporations. Like lumber.'

He talked about this for a long time – I can't remember if I was interested, but I was never bored. When you're doing shit you end up talking a lot of shit and it never matters what it's about – you just talk. We spent days, weeks being there and not there, floating on the ground, raving behind the curtains on sunny days. I would cue up the Revox, run another tape; Jules would chop it out on the coffee table, on the glass in the photo frames.

I liked railing up on the photographs, the bric-à-brac wash left by the years he and Candy had been together. Book spines, pop songs, ticket stubs – being in that room was like running my fingers through her hair. I was paying attention to every detail of it now: what they talked about, read, listened to, wore. I clung to everything that was theirs to lose or transfer.

Candy and I arranged to meet at the Normandy. She picked the venue.

I was a little shaky when I drove over, and the K Road end of town was starting to stink. Council workers hosed down the gutters on Sunday mornings but once a week wasn't enough in this heat. Even at ITD we had enough extra fans running to twice blow a fuse.

I parked in the gravel loading bay behind the Family & Naval and walked through the traffic jammed around the intersection. I was looking forward to having a beer to clear my head and the taste in my mouth. As usual, the curtain was drawn across the front door of the Normandy. I unhooked the little chain and walked inside.

Candy was sitting in a booth right by the door talking to a guy. She was facing me; I could only see his back. He had huge, broad shoulders and a black ponytail, like a sumo wrestler. He was resting his hands in front of him on the edge of the table. There was a ring on every finger.

Candy was wearing a sleeveless top zipped up to her throat. She must have seen me walking in but she didn't look up. She was doing a deal and didn't want to be interrupted. I didn't want to interrupt, either. I walked past, keeping my eyes on the counter. I got a beer and sat down in a booth at the other end of the room where my back was turned to them both. The beer did taste good.

She came over five minutes later holding an empty glass and an unlit cigarette. She dumped her purse on the table and slid into the seat. She always looked different in the daylight. Her skin was paler and she had freckles.

'It's good to see you,' she said.

'You want another beer?'

'Yeah. It's so damn hot.'

I went and got us two beers, glancing at her while I waited to be served. She lit her cigarette with a disposable lighter and returned it to her purse and leaned back. She was sitting with her knees touching and her feet apart, her needle toes pointed inward. She held her cigarette up by her face, her right elbow cupped in her left hand, the smoke wiggling. She was playing with the choker ring at her collar like she was going to unzip it because of the heat, but she didn't. She was staring into the middle of the room like it was a long way off.

I took the beers over and stood them on the table.

'Thanks,' she said and sipped it.

'I didn't know you came here,' I said.

'Everyone comes here. It's a small town. Everyone knows each other. Everyone's fucking.'

'Is everything okay?'

'Yeah, everything's cool. It's just the usual fucking shit. I'll sort it out.'

I glanced back. Her big friend with the ponytail had left.

'You want to go somewhere else?' I said.

'Where would we go?'

'Some place quiet.'

'I'd like to be somewhere without science,' she said, turning the bottle in its place like a dial. 'Where it's always sunset, you know?'

'You mean, getting out of it.'

She nodded. 'Being very, very high.'

'We could do that.'

'When don't we do that?'

I nodded. I could tell what was coming.

'Listen,' she said. 'At the consulate – I was wrong what I said about Jules. We made our decisions together.'

'That's what you wanted to tell me?'

'I don't know,' she said. 'I just didn't want to give you the wrong idea. I don't want to be bitter and twisted about this.'

'We're just having a drink.'

'We had a good time with that crowd,' she said. 'They were good to me. They were good to him. It's why he still hangs out with them. They're his past. He tries to carry them around. He loves the past – there's nothing wrong with that.'

'What about what's happening right now?'

'The present lasts between three and twelve seconds, did you know that? It's just a period in your brain.'

'That's some argument.'

'I'm just talking.'

'Cool.'

She blew smoke. 'So, are you busy at work?'

'Flat out. A whole lot of offices disappeared.'

She smiled. 'You're kidding.'

When the power cut out at the bottom of town the alarms crashed and the back-ups kicked in. But many of those systems were untested or ran off an old battery that only lasted a few hours, and when they failed the monitoring signals being sent to the security companies and the fire department ceased and the buildings themselves vanished from the screens. I counted the missing premises on my fingers.

'The ambulance stations vanished,' I said. 'The central police station lost its top floor. Shop managers have been getting daily pager messages telling them their place has burned down. The parking building under the Civic Theater comes and goes.'

'That's crazy.'

'It's a nightmare, is what it is.'

Candy liked that story. She rolled grey ash into the bottle neck and put the cigarette softly back between her lips. She was right about the past. We were all stuck with our memories. I was looking at her, still searching for the party girl I met in the hall, available and wide-eyed and warm with sweat.

'I think you're extraordinary,' I said.

'I won't help you get anything back, Sam.'

'Fair enough.'

'Jules likes you. I like you. We should be friends.'

It was hot in the booth. She twisted a cramp out of her neck, rubbing it. The seats made a popping noise as she shifted against the vinyl. She leaned across and cupped my hand and drew it close, pressing my knuckles into her stomach. She looked over my shoulder. I looked at the wall.

We stayed that way for a long time in the corner of the bar. We said nothing. The situation spoke for itself. Neither one of us was game to interrupt.

Chapter 7

I tried calling her a couple of times but got no reply. I tried not to think about it. I kept my head down. Work kept me busy.

Up at the Domain the War Memorial Museum lost five years. The systems had crashed a week before a new exhibition was due to open in the south wing.

'American Scientific Photography,' Raymond read from the brochure. 'A touring display of the images of the technological revolution. What a crock.'

The exhibition couldn't open until the venue complied with insurance regulations, which included working environmental controls and alarms – and the lights that would let people see it, Raymond chortled. He was walking around telling everyone this was going to pay for his retirement.

'Have you planned for your later years, Sam?' he said. 'Do you know what you're gonna do with yourself – where you'll live and who will pay for your meals and shit? You have to think about these things.'

He was eating a chicken sandwich. I could see the meat between his teeth.

'I thought I'd put you on it,' he said. 'You could get out, get a little fresh air. How would that be? You could employ some of your people skills.'

It sounded like sarcasm but he was actually trying to be nice. He even lent me his briefcase. I took the vodka bottle out of the bottom drawer and put it in the case and got in my car and drove up the hill.

The gardens around the Domain were bright with summer. The peaked roof of the building caught the sun. Tourist buses stopped along the forecourt and filled the front steps with tourists. I parked out back, by the service entrance.

It took a few hours to fix the system. The security guards gave me a place to work in one of the booths out back, brought me coffee. I had to go to the rest room a couple of times. They thought I was nervous.

I finished the work in time. Half an hour before sunset, as the guests were arriving in the pinking gardens I threw a switch and the outside spots came on, lighting up the columns like the Acropolis. There was scattered applause from the workers inside the little booth. One of the curators invited me to stay for the opening. I said I needed to go to the bathroom again, but I'd find my way.

The air inside the building smelled stale. It had the flavour of dust and wax and cold stone walls. It took my eyes a moment to adjust. At first I could make out the skylight, then the blue security fluorescents that marked out the walkways like a landing strip.

The place was slowly opening up, flickering. I started to orient myself, remembering the layout I'd seen on the monitors. And then I blinked. I could see dozens of pairs of black wings arched behind glass.

I was in the Bird Hall.

Inside the cabinets seagulls nested on a painted sand spit. A moa stood in a native forest. Tiny hummingbirds bobbed on curved wires, their soft bellies preserved in many different colours.

I followed the metal railing. Prehistoric crustaceans scuttled along the green sand. A squid and a blue whale hung on the wall. There was a shark with a white plaster belly and rows of teeth.

My footsteps clicked on the marble. The corridor broke off three ways. I could go into the Hall of Man or the Planetarium or the Egyptian Room. I could take something. I could set fire to the place. There was nothing to stop me. The guards weren't watching through the security cameras dotted around the ceiling: they were out parking cars. I had the whole place to myself.

In the blue light, everything was magical. Because there were no reflections in the glass, the wires supporting the exhibits became invisible. Stones and feathers floated in mid-air. There was no canned commentary. I stepped over the barriers. I touched a sword and a ceremonial dagger. I slipped a short blade out of its restraint. It was just waiting to be used again.

I stopped.

I could hear Jules. Talking to someone.

I held my breath. I put the dagger back in its cradle. The conversation was coming from the Planetarium. There was a light trap across the door. I slipped behind the curtain. The numbered seat rows counted down to the centre of the circular room where Jules stood by the star-projector, a black metal globe pitted with lenses and pinholes. He was talking to a man in a pale suit. I recognised the man's friendly smirk from the consulate. His name was Dedit something.

Jules' voice was shaking. Each time he spoke he banged the globe to make his point. The man was nodding patiently, like it was all rolling off his back.

'Didn't you explain?' Jules said.

'Of course I explained. They are all doing their best but they don't have your fine mind. You must realise, it's difficult for them to visualise.'

'Lars, nobody knows that better than I do.'

'Of course,' Dedit said.

'This isn't just anything.'

'Of course.'

'I can't pull it out of a hat. Have you told them that? Do they know that?'

'We have gone over this many times,' Lars said.

'I just keep saying it and saying it. Isn't anybody listening to what I'm saying?'

'We are all listening. We all hear it but please listen to what I am saying, Julian. I'm asking you to help me, also.'

'You know I want to help.'

'Of course. But we are all a step behind you. They are not so fast to work this out. And they know this. They acknowledge it. This is not pressure. That is the last thing they want. They know pressure won't help.'

'And — ?' Jules said.

Lars shrugged. 'They still want to see it.'

Jules slapped the machine again.

'Julian.'

'That's what they want, don't they?'

'Look, everything is important. But there comes a time when you must close a deal.'

'This is just a deal, to you.'

'Everything is a deal. Everything is a transaction. You cannot escape that. You are feeling the weight of this responsibility. So are they. You can't deny their request.'

'What, to show them something that isn't finished?'

'Not finished.' Lars tasted the words for the first time.

'We had a schedule,' Jules said. 'We had an agreement. It'll be ready at the time we agreed. So fuck them.'

'Please. Julian.'

'No. Fuck them. Tell them that.'

'They have made a big investment.'

'I needed that money to get started. That was part of the deal.'

'A lot of money. A gesture of faith.'

'So why don't you have faith in me?'

'Julian. I have faith in you. I know you'll come through. But my word is only so good.'

Jules was nervously playing with the projector's controls. He was speaking the same way he had written the notes up in the auditorium, overwriting the scratches of white chalk. Lars had got under his skin and they both knew it. He didn't know whether to stay or walk. He switched the constellations on. There was a low hum as the machine rotated and the stars rolled across the sky.

'What sign are you?' Lars said.

'What?'

'They have astrological signs.' He pointed. 'The twins . . . It's charming, don't you think? All this science with a little black magic. Everyone is superstitious, no matter who they are. We need to hold their hand. That is what I'm asking you to do.'

'You think what I'm doing is vapour.'

'Nobody has said this.'

'Maybe they're right,' Jules said.

Lars held up his hands. 'Calm yourself. This is about faith. Investors need something to believe in. When they lose faith, you need to show them something that restores that. All they are asking for is a reason to believe.'

Lars was sounding soothing but he wasn't moving an inch. Jules was breathing hard now. He cleared his throat and spat. He was hyperventilating and his stomach was jumping. Lars didn't figure it out until it was too late.

'Julian,' Lars said. 'Are you feeling unwell?'

Jules coughed and retched and threw up on the projector, his bile splattering across the mechanism.

'Fuck,' Lars said and turned towards the entrance for help. I got out before he could see me, retracing my steps towards the glass and cardboard beach.

The exhibition opening was well underway. The guests were talking among themselves and ignoring the photographs. I got myself a glass of wine and went to look the pictures over. Some I'd seen reproduced in books and magazines but the prints were smaller than I'd imagined. Up close, the grain of the film was visible, the paper buckling in its mount.

There was a naked woman riding a horse and two naked men wrestling, each movement captured second by second. Drops of milk falling and exploding into a microscopic coronet. A bullet at the moment it passed through a light bulb, the bulb mostly intact. Three balloons decaying as an arrow pierced them: the first shredded rubber, the second half-exploded, the third still whole.

A bullet cutting a playing card in half.

Dedit appeared and shook my hand.

'Lars Dedit,' he said. 'We met at the consulate. You are here with Jules?'

'No.' I looked around. 'Is he here?'

'He's in the men's room. Bad stomach – nerves, I think.' Lars handed me his business card. It was blank. I turned it over. There was nothing on the other side. I held it up to see the watermark: a fine L in the centre, and a phone number.

'We're lucky to be here, no?' Lars said. 'I heard they wouldn't be able to open after the power cut.'

'They must have fixed it.'

He pointed at the picture of the playing card shot in half. 'You get the joke?'

'No.'

'Look at the date: 1964. Jack Kennedy was shot in 1963. The card is the jack of diamonds. One year after Dealey Plaza. This photographer's work was funded by the American military. His little joke. Or maybe not a joke. Maybe he is trying to tell us something, yes? Who knows? A good story. Wine?' He grabbed one of the waiters and swapped his empty glass for three that were full. 'Take one.'

'I've already got one.'

'What do you know about moderation?' he winked. 'You're a friend of Jules. Have this and we will go and look for him.'

I didn't want to find Jules right now. I steered Lars back to the photographs. He pointed to a mushroom cloud billowing above a line of trees.

'How about this one?' he said. 'It's called "Tower Test". You take a photograph of a nuclear explosion, right? The explosion is naturally very bright, a nuclear flash. The exposure is standard. Along here – the parked vehicles, the little fake houses – that gives you distance, and distance gives you scale. With exposure and scale you can calculate the size of the blast. With a date, you can say what the military is testing, and when. This is why you test in the ocean, away from the cameras.'

'If that's true,' I said, 'why would they release any photos at all?'

'Because it's beautiful propaganda. These photographs say technology is wonderful, so why worry about anything? Technology will solve everything.' Lars tapped his two glasses so they chimed. 'It's a pretty thought, no?'

Chapter 8

Candy left a message on my answering machine. She gave an address on the west coast but no number, the hesitation sounding in her voice. I drove out there before either of us could think better of it.

The road was a narrow two-lane that twisted through the hills, the sun flashing at every turn. Thick bush ran along both sides of the highway, the cutting hiding the oncoming traffic. Accidents were a regular event out here. If a driver lost it on the camber a car would run off and roll down the bank without any trace of leaving the road. A wreck could lie unnoticed for days.

At the crest of the hills the road turned right and tipped down to the coast. The most expensive properties ran along this part of the cliff. Miami stucco and picture windows caught the sun and the roadside was busy with hidden driveways. By the time I reached the bottom of the hill the brakes smelled of burning rubber and the back of my shirt was stuck to the seat. The car radio was dead, the signal blocked by the shadow of the range.

The litter of three generations of low-rent holidays ran along the beach. Red, green and silver-patched iron roofs poked out of the trees. The lawns were interrupted by standing clothes-lines and old cars, surfboards and white mailboxes and cracked concrete water tanks.

I parked the car behind the dunes and got out and made my way on to the sand.

The coast was curving away, gradual and endless in the afternoon. The sand had baked to a hot crust that broke with each step. A strong breeze lifted a haze above the waves. There was a good three-foot surf. Lifesavers had planted flags in the shallows to mark where it was safe to swim. The surfers were paddling way out past the breakers, shining in their black wet suits like seals.

I kept walking. I tasted salt on the back of my hand. It took another good half-hour to reach the head of the beach. The rocks looked like a body lying on its side. People were climbing around it, exploring the caves.

I saw Candy. She was wearing a green army shirt with the sleeves rolled up. Her hair was in plaits and she was tanned. She was standing ankle-deep in a pool formed by the incoming surf, tearing pieces off a long roll of paper and dropping them into the water. When she saw me she stopped and let her arms fall, as if the paper roll had suddenly turned heavy.

'You made it,' she said. 'I thought you'd be working.'

'Things are pretty mad in town.'

'I heard the whole grid could come down.'

'That's the rumour.' I squinted at the breakers. 'Has it been like this every day?'

'Every day.' She shaded her eyes with her hand. 'The coast was one of the things I always remembered about New Zealand. The colour of the water – the turquoise. You don't get that anywhere else.'

The shreds of paper were floating on the meniscus of the tidal pool like leaves. I recognised them from the diagrams I'd found on her computer. She was tearing up the drawings for her blade.

'What are you doing?' I said.

She smiled at me with her mouth but not her eyes. The roll flapped and folded in the wind. She ripped the last piece in half and let it fall.

She was staying at an old weatherboard place a few steps behind the dunes. The ranch slider was open and a towel was drying on the porch rail. A pump house stood out back on an unmown lawn. A single black electrical wire ran from the bush to the house on a T-pole but there was no phone line.

'You have to call from the store,' she said. 'The owner teaches sitar – he's from Pakistan. He put a satellite dish in his backyard. He's got a hundred channels and a pay phone on the counter.'

'How long have you had this place?'

'It was my grandmother's. It used to be further back. The whole foreshore's moving. The sand blows in and thins the forest and then that destabilises the hill, so when the rains come in winter, the slips cover the sand again. It might not be here in thirty years. Then again, it could be.'

The bach was a single room with a bed to one side. White patches of light fell across the papers on the dining table and the battered computer in the corner. At the back was a sink set in a narrow bench and a ghetto blaster on the window-sill. The single bookshelf had no books on it. It was lined with shells and old bones bleached by the sea. The place smelled of salt and Coppertone and sandalwood and the wind-dried cotton sheets on the bed and the dust of old cushions faded by years of holidays.

Now I was inside, I realised how noisy the sea had been. I was tired from walking. My neck itched and my skin felt thick.

'Sit down,' she said. 'Take your shirt off. You look like you're going to faint.'

I unbuttoned my collar. 'I have to keep my shoulder out of the sun.'

'What, for ever?'

'For a couple more years. Until the scar's older.'

She put a Johnny Cash tape on and carried out a tray with a frozen bottle of vodka and two shot glasses and two glasses of lemonade. The alcohol tasted like pepper with the weight of syrup and the lemonade pricked my eyes. She refilled the shots and we drank again.

'Why were you tearing up your work?'

'It's already torn up,' she said. 'It doesn't work.'

'You said it was going well.'

'Everything's based on a set of calculations I made

when I first started, years ago. But this week I started the final cut and it doesn't work.'

'What do you mean?'

'The surfaces contradict each other.' She rubbed her forehead. 'The original calculations show that the two opposing edges of the blade will move through the water just right. The only problem is that when I draw them in a real space, they don't meet up.'

'So you have to start again.'

'I can't start again. I need a supercomputer to do that. But the closest one to here is in a naval laboratory in Maui – it'd cost a fortune. I don't have any backers.'

'Get the navy to sponsor it.'

'I don't want to do that. I don't want my work sponsored by the military. But until I can book time, I'm fucked. I've been sitting around pretending I'm finishing the details but really I'm not doing anything. It's ridiculous. After all this time, I've been working on a blade with two edges that don't meet.'

She rubbed the lines under her eyes.

'I've been asking myself why I came back,' she said. 'How I ended up living alongside the people here. There's a crazy old woman next door, and an old hippy guy with a dog. Beach people. They've been here their whole lives and now I've just washed up alongside them with the driftwood. I should have stayed in New York. I should have been someone else.'

'Like who?'

'Someone stronger. Anyone,' she said. 'Did you bring anything with you, Sam?'

'Sure. You want something?'

'Thanks.'

I set it out by the sink, Johnny Cash singing 'Ring of Fire'. I called her in. Afterwards we put the chairs out on the porch to watch the sea pounding a hard white line along the bay.

The horizon ripened and bruised and then it was night. The lights of the houses draped themselves along the hill. The ice on the vodka bottle melted into a pool. The lemonade ran out. The warm alcohol tasted sharp. We stopped talking. Even wired up, we couldn't find the conversation we'd had at the consulate. She cradled the shot in her genius hands and chewed her plait, her jaw working.

We listened to the same tape a couple of times before she got up to change it. I followed her. She ejected the cassette. I put my arms around her and kissed the back of her neck. She didn't blink. She leaned back into me. I slid my hands under her shirt, felt her stomach. She breathed a little more deeply and let her head fall to the side. She smelled of tanning lotion and sweat. She put her hands on my pockets. I pushed up her shirt and it fell back and open at her neck, and I saw the tattoos.

The ink ran the length of her spine and wider: small, spidery letters like marks on a school desk. I touched the first:

$$c = \sqrt{gh}$$

C is wave speed. H is water depth. G is gravity. I touched the next.

$$\frac{L}{\sqrt{gh}}$$

'Reflection of a wave in a closed basin.'

'That's right,' she whispered.

'When did you get these?'

'I got the first one in New York. A Spanish guy with turtleshells and fifties pin-up girls on the wall. He used special needles to get it so fine. He played wrestling videos while he did it.'

I touched her spine. It was black. Her muscles flexed. Science rose and fell with her breathing.

'I was arguing with Jules,' she said. 'Lively debate, he would call it. Mathematics is the science of war and war is the science of mathematics – has he told you that one? I said he was wrong. He said I was stupid to pursue my work, that I was an idealist. He said I didn't believe in what I was doing. That's when I got the first one. To prove what I believed in.'

'And the others?'

'Wherever we stopped. When I got bored. When I couldn't concentrate – when I had to think about my work.'

'How many are there?'

'I lost count. Don't you like them?'

She was gently bending forward over the bench sink, letting me inspect beneath her waistband.

'Some of them are pretty rough.'

'I haven't always gone to professionals.'

Some of them didn't look like tattoos. She put her chin in her hands while I stroked and felt the breaks in the flesh: the reddened hash marks that ticked off the years before now, before we met. I had arrived too late to understand it. It had been written for someone else.

We fucked on the floor by the bed, Candy reaching up to clench the sheets, my legs scraping on the wood. She banged her head and I bruised my arms. It felt like a fight. We pushed, rocking from side to side. She struggled sideways, crab-inching across the carpet. She shuddered and broke away and came back. We continued until we were exhausted. I held her. She pushed me away.

We didn't sleep and we didn't talk. We just lay there until the sun came up. Her tan turned pale in the dawn. Her breath stuck under her fingernails. I touched her tattoos again but she was colder now. We were coming down fast – a long way down. She climbed up on the bed and pulled herself under the sheets. I railed up by the shells and bones, just enough for the drive back into town. She was asleep when I slid the ranch slider shut.

Out in the shallows, the sun had turned the tide pools pink and red. As I crossed them I felt a rasp in my chest. There was nothing to be had out here: nothing to regain. When I looked back the waves had smoothed over even my footprints. The beach had become long and curved, honed by forgetting.

Chapter 9

I was driving into the city when the second cut hit. First the traffic signals failed and then the fire alarms went off. From my car I saw no lights in the windows. The air-conditioning had stopped and moving lifts had stuck between floors. Illuminated signs blanked.

People started pouring out of the buildings. The glass doors wouldn't open and had to be pushed apart. Workers climbed out on the fire escapes. They assembled on each street corner, smoking, passing around mobile phones. A police helicopter approached and started circling overhead. Drivers pulled out of the traffic jam and cut their engines.

It was oddly quiet. The sirens on the fire-tenders responding to alarms could be heard from a long way off, wavering in quality as they weaved through the streets. The firemen had to get out and run along the footpaths, their boots pounding under the weight of equipment protecting them from flames that weren't burning.

The city's power was travelling along four cables less than six feet below the ground. Over decades the surrounding clay had shrunk in summer and swelled in winter, twisting each line until it looked like a worm dried out on the sidewalk. Two of the lines were gas-insulated and two were suspended in oil, and where those lines had bent the liquid was seeping into the ground.

The system had continued to work because the load was shared evenly across four cables. But now one had been cut, the power being carried by the remaining three had increased to the point where they were beginning to fail. The system was going down. It was this second cut that did the real damage. It was like lightning had struck twice, a black fork sucking everything back up into the sky.

When I finally threaded my way through the traffic to ITD I couldn't get into the parking building. The yellow ticket arm had locked across the exit and the drivers inside were backed up through three levels. I left my car in a towaway zone and went in through the fire entrance. The lights were still on and the card swipe still worked. The building had its own generator. The soda in the fridge would still be cold.

The incoming boxes were stacked to the ceiling. The desk in my office was already surrounded. I sat down and started working. There was sand under my fingernails.

It was crazy. It had all failed. Systems hadn't recovered from the first strike. People had no back-up. They weren't expecting this to happen.

Getting around the city had become a major problem. Traffic signals blacked out. Cars overheated and broke down. The delays spread outwards fast to reach the motorway ramps and the bridge, causing accidents. Ambulances were called out, and got stuck. More people were parking on the street, narrowing the lanes. More streets blocked.

People tried to keep working. Businesses started sending everything by courier. The couriers sent cyclists. Because elevators weren't working, the deliveries had to go by the stairs. Visitors had to call to get someone to come down and unlock the door. Phones started to ring off the hook.

Restaurants and hotels and bars refused to close. Summer was when they made most of their annual profit. They used diesel generators to power the lights and refrigerators. If they didn't have a genera-tor on-site they picked up the phone and ordered one from a hire pool, and the hire pool put the generator on a delivery truck and drove into town.

The mayor told people to stay out of the city. The casual traffic started to empty out. The only people left were the ones who were panicking.

Everyone at ITD was smiling, of course. This was how we made our money. Only the clients were pissed. Raymond hired a temp so she and Holly could take turns being shouted at. Raymond insti-tuted our own method of back-ups which in turn had to be monitored, and soon anyone who could count on their fingers was complaining that trying to save everything and keep track of it was doubling the time it took to finish a job, then doubling it again.

That raised voices inside the building, not just on the phone. A box got slammed down just hard enough to stop the giggling. So Raymond organised a shipment of a little something for everyone as a gratuity, plus a discount for future orders, and that cheered us back up for a while.

We were working around the clock. I was burning up my own supply as well as anything Raymond brought in. The washing machine and the TV weren't working at my apartment so I stopped going home. I stayed at the office and put in the hours. If I wanted to sleep, I went out to the car, but only during the day. At night the streets outside were empty and it was easier to work.

Because we had to get it all done. We had to grab contracts before they went to anyone else. It was like fishing in the ocean when a big catch comes through: it was pay day, and we could all smell the money. I needed it. Between Raymond's orders and mine I was running up big bills.

Raymond couldn't stop grinning. He believed that two or three people working together can be as smart as a single person, and four would be smarter as a group than as individuals, but once it got to thirty-five it crossed to the other side of the curve where people got a lot dumber. Any organisation, no matter how smart, looked like cattle to him. You gave the workers the money and powder they needed to get the job done and they would work until they dropped.

I couldn't argue with him. I would have said he

respected me more than he respected the other employees, but really Raymond didn't respect anyone. He was riding the wave and his boys were rubbing their faces, swearing – the nervous tics from chemicals and no sleep. We needed drugs. We couldn't take a break. It was the only way we could keep up.

The power companies had stopped trying to predict what would happen next. They ran pictures in the newspapers showing the city blocked out in different sections dimming from white to grey to black like states in a doomed continent. Everyone knew it was going to fuck up. It wasn't a case of how, just when.

The businessman's hotel bookings for his mistress: I left those corrupted. The solicitor hoarding porn files I let off the hook. The fake accounts, the angry letters – I gave them all another chance. Normally I would have dug them up and left them out for others to see, but not this month. I had vodka and a shaving mirror. I shut my door and took the phone off the hook.

I got a postcard in the mail. It carried no message. It was a picture from the photography exhibition: the first and only atomic bomb built before the one that was dropped on Japan. It showed the bomb inside a tent, wired up with triggers and monitoring equipment, a big black eight-ball about to disappear in a light brighter than the desert sun. Skinny men in uniform were clambering around in the shade, their faces airbrushed into grey.

Candy and Jules led lives too different from mine. I didn't expect to see them again. I was surprised when Holly came in and told me Jules was on the line.

'Did you get my postcard?' he said.

'I did.'

'Pretty cool, don't you think?' He sniffed. 'It's from that exhibition.'

'I recognise it.'

'I can't believe I missed you that night. Where are you now?'

'I'm at work. At the number you called.'

'What are you doing?'

'Working.'

'You?' There was a smile in his voice.

'It's been known.'

'Me too. I get to the end of the day and I don't know what I've been doing,' he said.

'That's how it is.'

'Listen, I need to ask you about something.'

'What?'

He paused. 'Are you sure I haven't already asked you about it?'

'I don't think so. Have you?'

'That's what I'm asking,' he said.

I could hear ice tinkling in a glass.

I looked out the window. It was hot out there. I had been inside for so long I'd stopped thinking about the weather. It had become just another thing that passed by the window with the pedestrians.

'I need a holiday,' I said. 'I'm starting to lose track of shit.'

'Where would you go?'

'Anywhere.'

'And what would you do there? Watch TV? Give your friends a call?'

'Maybe I would. I don't know.'

'Seriously,' Jules said. 'What's left for you to do in the world? Everything's taken care of. It's all right here.'

'Listen, I'd better go.'

'Sammy? I need a favour.'

'What?'

'I need your help with something.'

'What is it?'

'I need some of your time.'

'I don't have any.'

'I want you to be part of something. I need your mind-space.'

'I can't come over right now,' I said. 'It's a bad time.'

It was a dumb excuse but it was the truth. I wanted to be prevented from seeing him. There wasn't enough distance between Jules and Candy and the woman I had touched.

'I could do with a hand, Sam.'

'Sure, but not now. I can't now.'

'Please think about it. Please consider. There's

something I need you to look at. Something I'm doing – all it will take is a little time.'

'What is it?'

'Some numbers. Why are you being a stranger?'

'I'll do it. But not now.'

'I'm disappointed, Sam.'

He paused like there was something else to say but there wasn't. Nothing came. I killed the line.

Chapter 10

Holly was chewing gum and wearing a dress that was inappropriate for the office.

'There's a message for you,' she said. 'Jules Way.'

'I just spoke to him.'

She looked at me while I thought about it. Did Jules call just now or was that yesterday? Was it two days ago? I wasn't sure.

'When did you last go home?' she said.

'Fucked if I know.'

I put the phone back on the hook and took my mobile out of the drawer and switched it on. It rang with a dozen messages. I flicked through them. The last was from a Dr Hayden. The number was an extension at Auckland Hospital.

I got Holly to call back. She got Hayden on the line and I hit the speaker button so I didn't have to pick it up.

'It's about a patient,' Dr Hayden said. 'Mr Julian Way. Do you know him?'

Jules was lying in a ward on a life-support machine.

Hayden told me where to find her at the hospital. I thanked her and put down the phone. I told Holly I was going out.

★ ★ ★

It was a long time since I'd driven to the hospital but the route came back to me quick. The motorway exit ramp ran along the back of a domestic street. The houses were on long sections with tall fences and shaggy backyards. Clay streaks marked where the second car or the dinghy trailer was parked over winter. Now the yellowing grass had been decorated with summer things: swings, a tricycle, a low stack of timber. You never saw people inside. It was like the noise of the motorway had pushed them out.

I pulled into the hospital grounds and parked out back and found my way through the corridors to the reception area. Patients were scattered around the foyer: a teenager with a bandaged head, a boy with a broken arm; grandchildren running around a big woman on crutches. A couple, both in wheelchairs, feebly held hands. I couldn't tell if they were being checked in or out. They looked like they all had been there for ever.

The nurse on the front desk wouldn't answer my questions, either because she wasn't allowed to or because she didn't know. She got sniffy when I complained about waiting so I backed off and slipped past the security door when she wasn't looking. I would find Hayden myself. I had an idea where a duty doctor might be.

The corridors were sunny and wide. People's shoes squeaked on the linoleum as they passed. An abandoned cleaning trolley was a landmark between wards that otherwise looked the same. I kept walking. The passages narrowed and got a little darker. The fewer windows in a ward, the less talking there was to be heard.

I wiped my palms on my shirt.

The buildings circled a courtyard. Sure enough, Hayden was standing outside by the rose garden, smoking with some of the nurses. She was short, with a blue cardigan and her hair pinned back with plain wire clips. I introduced myself. She gave me a look like she was in the middle of a day that was getting harder to deal with, and the nurses gave her a look like being interrupted was all you could expect to happen.

She dropped her cigarette under her shoe and clutched the soft pack and the lighter in her cardigan pockets as she showed me back inside. We talked about the no-smoking rules and how patients would join the nurses in the courtyard or the car park, and how people who weren't hospital workers got upset about it.

'You obviously know someone who works in health care,' she said.

'I used to.'

'Are you all right? You look pale.'

'It's getting the news.'

'You never get used to it.'

'You mean I'm going to hear it more than once?'

I meant it as a joke but it didn't come out like one and she didn't laugh.

Her office was small with a wide pine desk that only just fitted between the wall and the frosted windows that looked out on to a misty corridor. She said she had to pull Jules' file and offered to bring me coffee on the way back but I said no thanks. I opened up the filing cabinet while I waited for her and flicked through it. There was a lot of paperwork inside: spreadsheets, forms, budgetary stuff.

I slid the drawer shut as she walked back in. I don't know if she saw me snooping. She didn't say anything if she did. She was carrying a white envelope and a manila folder and two polystyrene cups swollen with hot coffee.

'I got you some anyway,' she said. 'Sugar?'

'Black is fine.'

She dropped three sugar sachets in front of me on the desk and we sat down.

'Thank you for coming in,' she said.

'It was a surprise.'

'I'm sure. I'm sorry about what's happened.'

We were both trying to peel the plastic lids off the cup without spilling any.

'So what happened to Jules?' I said. 'Where is he?'

'Still in intensive care. There's been no change since the police brought him in. He was found unconscious in the street, in the central city. He'd been assaulted. There's extensive trauma to the head. I don't know if you're aware of his drug use.'

She made it sound bland. I broke a sachet and tipped the sugar into my coffee, nodding slowly. I figured the pharmaceutical supply room was three floors above us and about a hundred yards back.

'Which drugs?' I said.

'He was positive for everything we tested for and

his blood alcohol was high. That's been a factor in the trauma. May I show you?'

She swivelled the folder around and showed me through the notes: the patient's condition on being admitted; the doctors' initial and ongoing reports; the recorded patterns from an ECG.

'The signs are that electrical activity in the brain is suppressed,' she said. 'Limited physical responses indicate that there may not be enough living cells in the brain to support conscious functioning. The signs are that death by complication is the most likely outcome.'

I couldn't think of what to say. There was nothing to say. It was just another fact, as plain as her sitting on the other side of the desk. Just like that.

'It's difficult, I know,' she said.

'And he gave you my name?'

'He was unconscious. But he was carrying this.' She slid the white envelope across the table. It had been addressed to me at work. 'You're the first person we've contacted.'

'Have you told his girlfriend?'

'The police haven't said anything about that.'

'Police?'

'They'll want to speak to you, of course.'

The inked lettering had got damp and soaked into the paper. I turned the envelope over. It was still sealed. Hayden watched it with as much curiosity as I did.

'It is addressed to you,' she said.

'I feel like I should see him first.'

She could have said that was a sentimental gesture, but she didn't.

Jules was being monitored in a sealed, air-conditioned ward. I stood listening to the machines click and whirr with the envelope in my hands: my name as he'd written it.

He looked like he was sleeping but his chest rose and fell in the shade of several pieces of equipment. It was strange how many devices were needed to reproduce simple breathing. His cheeks were swollen and his lips were grey. The bruises had an unchanged quality. The tube in his throat was taped with an X, like something had been buried there.

Our memories have no clear edges. Scenes from the past shift like clouds, obscured by glial veils. The line between what happened and what we imagined has to be read in the half-light of synapses. It has to be clarified, propped up by photographs and sticky yellow notes. And then a smell or a sound, and it all comes back.

I remembered staring at the tiled ceiling as they wheeled me in. The sound of sliding curtains and nurses talking, the rubber bed sheet, the hard plastic edges of the surgical trays. Nurses walked quickly around the circle of beds. They peeled back the soiled gauze and removed the drip the ambulance men had inserted and dropped it in a black plastic bag.

They inserted a new needle. I didn't know what they were giving me. I was saying: no drugs.

Nothing. I waved my hand in case they couldn't understand what I was saying. The movement pushed the needle out and warm blood ran down my wrist. One of the nurses held me down while the other put it back in.

I remembered the clear face-mask. A sterile packet torn and shaken out. Sutures. They moved fast, with deliberate ease, calm purpose and clarity, swabbing blood the way you dust a table, cleaning a hole in living flesh. You were broken and they fixed you, a mess they cleaned up. Busy talking, saving a life, moving on.

I was thinking: please don't call her. Don't go back to the apartment.

No drugs, please.

I knew I was living a short life. I knew suffering would catch up but I never counted on this: the silence and the stale air and artificial lights and walls the colour of surrender.

I opened the envelope. The letter was a single sheet of onion-skin, translucent in the lights. At the top of the page were the words *anyway freedom* and at the bottom was *goodbye*, and the rest was all numbers. Tiny numbers shaped like the writing on a woman's back, but they weren't formulae: just single digits stacked like the windows in a skyscraper.

A tear was running from Jules' closed eye. Hayden checked the ventilator.

'His eye's watering. I've seen it before. The

lacrimal duct contracts and squeezes out a tear. It's not a conscious action.'

'It's normal?'

'With a coma, yes. I wouldn't draw anything from it.'

It was scary to wake up with a tube down your throat but that wasn't going to happen. The bandage around his head was clean. Someone would change the dressing every day.

'So how long does this go on for?' I said.

'We'll continue to monitor him. But there's been no variation in the data. The chances are very low.'

'Do you know what Cherenkov radiation is?'

'No, I'm sorry.' She checked her watch. 'Do you know his girlfriend's phone number?'

'She's out at the beach. There's no phone. I should tell her.'

'And we're required to notify the police that you've been here.' She hesitated.

'I'll leave my number.'

'The police will contact his partner as well.'

'No. I'll do it.'

'The police will probably want to read the letter.'

'Yes.'

Like it would tell them anything.

Chapter 11

I drove out to the coast practising the words under my breath. He is in the hospital. He is going to die. I wasn't good at saying it. Sunlight flashed through the scrub like bad news coming down the wire. It would have been easier to let the cops and doctors handle it. This was their job, after all, but I didn't want them to be the ones to tell her. With the words, I was reciting Candy Strange to myself. Lettered skin and Chinese collar. I was doing the right thing for the wrong reason.

I knew to park further down the beach this time but it was still a long walk across the sand. When I reached the house it was closed up and the blinds were drawn. I knocked on the ranch slider. There was no reply. I went around the back and looked in the windows but saw no movement. The pump house was locked up. She was out.

I waited on the porch for a long time but there was no sign of her returning. I found a piece of wood and broke a pane in the back door as gently as I could and flipped the latch, calling her name as I crunched the glass underfoot. The computer was gone and the kitchen bench was clean. The bed had been stripped. Dust had already started to settle on the shells and bones in the bookcase. The place had been closed up with half of summer to come. The trash had been taken out but things still smelled bad.

I walked back to my car, the sun burning my forehead pink. I put on *Stellar Regions* and drove back fast, consoling myself with Coltrane and speed.

My phone woke up as I got closer to town. I answered but it was only Raymond asking where I was. I made excuses. Work was flooding in so it was best to stay away as long as possible. I called the hospital and asked if Candy was there but she hadn't visited. I made my way to the apartment thinking maybe it wasn't too late.

Beaten and left for dead.

Their apartment building seemed smaller against the skyline. The front door had been wedged open and a notice taped to the glass that said Our power is OUT you cannot be BUZZED IN I am in the GARDEN. Inside it was musty and cool. The elevator gate was padlocked. The sun shining at the rear of the foyer picked out the worn pattern in the carpet, the weave of strangers' footsteps. I could hear a petrol engine rattling behind the glass doors.

I knocked and a thin old man opened them up. The pushed-up sleeves of his bush shirt showed the grey hair on his forearms. His checked pants were tucked into gumboots flecked with cement and his half-frame spectacles were hanging on a cord around his neck.

Behind him, the courtyard was criss-crossed by

planks balanced on shaky combinations of bricks. Underneath, the ground had been dug up and sculpted into terraces boxed with scoria and chicken-wire. The engine noise was coming from a mixer bucking its frame like a dog on a leash.

I shouted that I wanted to get inside. He shook his head and stomped across the planks to cut the engine. The courtyard fell quiet. Between each step he paused to miss the spring in the boards, the wary walk of an old man. He pulled off his green rubber gloves and put on his spectacles and raised his chin to introduce himself, a drop of sweat wobbling on the tip of his nose.

'George Saddler,' he said. 'Are you from the insurance company?'

'Pardon me?'

'You've come about the damage in 12B?'

'I've come to see one of the owners – Candy Strange. What do you mean, damage?'

He blinked. 'There's been a power cut. Every appliance in the building stopped working. The fridge in 12B defrosted and the water got everywhere – ruined the carpet. I had to clean the place. The tenants weren't there. I don't know where they are. Did they send you?'

'No. I came to see them.'

'Haven't seen them in a while. You should've smelled the place. I had to get people in, y'see.'

'Right.'

'Four hundred, it cost. Hell of a mess.'

'So you haven't seen either of them?'

96

'Not for a while, no.'

'I don't know if I'm the person to tell you this, Mr Saddler –'

'George.'

'George. My name's Sam.'

'How'd you do.' He shook my hand.

'Pleased to meet you. Listen, Jules is in hospital.'

'That explains the fridge going off like that.'

'And I came to see Candy, to check that she's okay.'

'He was a scientist of some sort,' George said.

'Mathematician.'

'I remember telling him, you shouldn't be a scientist, you should be a plumber. The world's full of scientists and professors but I can't get a damn plumber when I need one, I recall advising him.'

'I guess he stuck with what he knew.'

'Plumbers and mechanics, that's what I know. People who do the work. You look like the sort of bloke who isn't afraid to get his hands dirty.'

'I was wondering if I could go up and check the apartment. Maybe I could leave a note or something.'

'You're a friend of hers, are you?'

'I know them both.'

'I've paid for all the work on the place,' he said.

'I can pick that up for them.'

'It's no worry for you, is it?'

'They can pay me back.'

'Saddler's got two d's.'

He had a crumpled invoice waiting in his shirt

97

pocket. I wrote him a cheque and he noted the spelling before unfolding a used envelope and shaking two brass keys out of it.

'So is he going to be okay, your friend?'

'I don't know.'

'The small key's for downstairs,' he said. 'We have to be safe, with no power.'

'It's good you've got that engine,' I said. 'You've got your work cut out.'

'The earth was fallow. Nothing grew here.'

'Couldn't you have brought it back?'

'Not now.' He pointed at the new apartment tower that rose behind us, its roof crested with TV and microwave aerials. 'They built that three years ago. The whole place has been in shade since then. We've got damp all round the back. Some of the people on the lower levels don't get any light at all after midday.'

'That's terrible.'

'Blackouts in the middle of summer.' He shook his head. 'You know what's wrong with this city? It's too damn complicated. Auckland was never meant to be the size it is now. We're on a tiny part of a tiny island and we're filling it up, packing more people in – one day it's going to crack up and slide back into the sea.'

He pointed at the new tower: 'Do you know what a place like that costs? You can't imagine. It's ridiculous. The only sort who can afford places like that are prostitutes and drug dealers. Who else can pay the rents? We're building a city for criminals.'

He squinted at the antennas on the skyline.

'What's all that radiation doing to you? Road-works running cables by the drinking water, the chemicals they put into it. No wonder blokes like your friend are getting sick. People don't care. Work's all that matters nowadays. That's all people worry about.'

'I guess,' I said.

Saddler sighed. 'Your friend was quiet. I didn't talk to him much. But he seemed like a fair enough sort of bloke. Don't take offence. I'm not talking about him.'

'No worries.'

He shuffled back across the planks and put the mixer back in gear. The engine coughed, raising a blue cloud of smoke. I looked at the maze of scoria and mud.

'So will this be a Zen garden or something, when it's finished?' I shouted.

Saddler blinked. 'Does it look Zen?'

I unlocked the downstairs door and took the stairs. Twelve flights up, I was puffing. The landing smelled of fluoron. I knocked and called Candy's name but there was no answer so I used the key. The stink of refrigerator fluid was stronger inside. The wet carpet had been peeled back in a roll to dry. The kitchen linoleum had been torn up and stacked in a corner. There was a black square of cockroach dirt on the floorboards.

I called her name again, just in case she was

sleeping. I pushed open the bathroom door. I went into the bedroom. Her things had gone. The dresser was empty and the drawers had been cleaned out. There were dust marks on the shelves where her things had been sitting. Nothing was broken. She had packed calmly and left. Jules' clothes were alone in the wardrobe: empty shirts, the jacket arms hanging limp.

The lounge was clean and the furniture was straight, which made it seem larger. She'd removed the photographs of herself before standing the empty frames back in their original positions on the shelf. The Revox was still set up. I flicked through the jazz tapes. I picked up the souvenir paperweights and shook each one in turn to watch its glitter fall in the afternoon sun. Cairo, Christmas Island, Cayenne. That was the joke, of course. They were snow-shakers for places where it didn't snow.

I looked around one last time, just to be sure, but I knew the letter was all I had left now, the onion-skin stacked with numbers. *Anyway freedom goodbye.* Every day you leave and then one day you don't come back. The air inside the apartment sounded like a record still turning after the song had finished, the needle crackling in the groove.

I dropped Saddler's keys in the letter-box on my way out.

Chapter 12

I called the number on Lars Dedit's business card. He was staying at the Viscount, a new place above Orakei Basin. His suite was on the top floor. The wide-screen TV was set into a curved cedar wall and the terrace balcony looked out over the pool and the harbour below. The glass dining table was covered in photographs. Lars sat me down while he opened the black mini-bar. His tan looked darker in the daylight.

'So what do you think of this place?' he said. 'I can't decide.'

'Pretty flash.'

'It's number eight. There are seven others around the world and they are all exactly the same on the inside, like aeroplanes.'

'That's how they do it now, I guess.'

'I see so many hotels. Cigarette?' He unwrapped a fresh pack. He set an iced bottle and tumblers on the glass. He poured the drinks and slid mine over and sat down, smoothing his tie.

'To friends,' he said. 'I am truly sorry to hear the news.'

'It's not good.'

'You've been to the hospital? You've seen him?'

I nodded. Lars winced.

I looked at the photographs on the table. They were glossy black and white panoramas gridded with crosses like the astronauts' pictures of the moon. It took me a moment to recognise the uneven patterns as vegetation and the arrhythmic white capillaries as engineered roads. They were satellite pictures of a coastline, its littoral milk dissolving to grey.

'You like them?' he said.

'They're beautiful. Where is it?'

'An island in the Pacific.'

'And you sell these?'

'On commission, yes. My company leases the orbit of the satellite and sub-lets it to clients. This gives them rights to all images and data collected across that period and distance.'

'Who are your clients?'

'Some government corporations, and private companies – agricultural planners, oil and mining companies, engineers. It's growing all the time. There is a big market for weather and tides. This one is French. One-metre resolution, the best.'

He found a print and tapped a matching pair of birds above a wave, one black and one white.

'See? This pale bird is the seagull, and this dark bird is its shadow on the water. Impressed? This is military quality. The trick is the resolution; how you compress the images and transmit them. You can filter an image for heat or radiation. It used to be that only the Americans and the Russians had this kind of technology but after the wall came down it all opened up.'

I helped myself to another drink. The vodka had a greasy surface on it, like oil.

'How do you mean, opened up?' I said.

'Now many countries have satellites. Government ments pay for their space programmes by leasing out their orbit. But also they have national security interests, so how much they lease out depends on the relationship they have with other countries. If there is an argument they pull out the whole rug no matter what the deal is. You can't get insurance for this. I am forever calling up foreign offices, trying to patch things up. These are very powerful bureaucracies. They move slowly, layers and layers of people making decisions. You think you have something signed and then suddenly a government changes and everyone is out and you have to start all over again.'

I flicked through the prints like they were giant playing cards.

'It's such a calm view of the world,' I said. 'It's so peaceful.'

'If you listen to the signal when it comes in from the satellite, over the speaker, the transmission is just noise. There is no shape to it: just speckled grey, static. The data has to be processed. Jules was working on what we call a new lens: algorithms to extract more detail from the images. Two, three times the quality. This was a very powerful tool, like being able to fly very high and zoom in suddenly on anything, like a bird. It would change our view of the world.'

'I wish I could have talked to him about it.'

'He never told you anything?' Lars said.

'Nothing.'

'You're friends. You never discussed it?'

'Never. I'd recall. We talked about a lot of things. Bombs and music.'

'Interpolation?'

'Vaguely.'

'Please. If you could wrack your brain, search back, anything. I would love to recover what has been lost.'

'That's the trick, isn't it?'

Lars sighed. He clasped the back of my hand.

'I am sorry,' he said.

'That's okay.'

'There are investors, a lot of money involved. And now, what do I tell them? I apologise. Sorry, Sam. Friends and business. It's remarkable how much you can lose.'

I snapped my fingers. 'Just like that.'

'You look tired.'

'I'm very tired.'

'How about I give you a little something to pick you up?'

'That would be great.'

He unfolded a square of paper and tapped out the powder on the glass and then took out a little stone point the shape and colour of an autumn leaf.

'Eighty thousand years old,' he said. 'You know

how cavemen made these? They took a piece of flint and hammered it with a bone until it became this fine and wonderful thing. This is the art that separates us from the animals.'

He divided the powder in three strokes.

'To friends,' he said again.

We got a table in the hotel restaurant just as the waiters were about to close up. We ordered three kinds of wine and whole fish and artichokes and didn't eat any of it.

'I'm trying to find Candy,' I said.

'You've spoken with her?'

'I don't know where she is. She's gone. Her things aren't in the apartment. The police will be looking for her.'

'She left the country,' Lars said.

'People are going to be asking me why.'

Lars glanced up at me. 'Then these people must respect what she's done. They must give her the benefit of the doubt. Truthfully – please, excuse me saying this now – I don't know if her leaving would have made a difference to him. He didn't value her. They cared for each other, I think, but he maintained a certain rank.'

'Jules, you mean.'

'Who else would I be speaking about?'

'I want to try and find her before anything happens at the hospital.'

'Before it ends.'

'If I could, yes.'

Lars was fidgeting with the spearhead, tapping it on the tablecloth.

'An archaeologist gave me this,' he said. 'My satellites found a very old road in Africa. He'd been searching for it for years. All we had to do was fly over once. It's a remarkable feeling, being the first to see something. That doesn't happen so often in a big country. Thirty, forty million people – you make no difference. You have to get philosophical. You give up. But here, on an island, the world doesn't overwhelm you. You believe everything you do matters.'

'You can still fuck things up.'

'It's true, there are stupid people out there,' he said. 'But one system fails, another replaces it. Nature isn't a continuum. It's about instability, upheaval. We have clients and suppliers all over the world, and there is conflict between borders – that's natural. All you can do is keep channels open, stay close to everyone.'

'Jules loved chaos. That's what brought us together.'

'Do you believe in predestination?'

'No.'

'Neither do I.'

I was thinking about Jules lying on his bed, in the half-light.

'Do you know Schrödinger's Cat?' I said.

'I've heard of it.'

'It's a paradox of quantum mechanics. There's a cat in a box with a gun pointed at it and the shot is triggered by the weight of a single atom. If the gun doesn't go off, the cat lives. If the shot is fired, the cat dies. But quantum theory says every atom exists simultaneously in decayed and undecayed states. So the gun fires and the gun doesn't fire and the cat exists in two states, simultaneously: alive and dead.'

Lars nodded. He didn't say if he got it. He just sat and listened and let me talk.

We ordered whisky and coffee and some exotic liqueur that appealed to his connoisseur's palate. We talked about Jules a little more and Candy not at all because she was at the front of both our minds. There was a piece of the story he knew and wasn't telling and I knew he didn't want to be pressed about it any more than I wanted to talk about what happened at the beach. So we both took the easy way out, picking at food that was soft to chew while our secrets darkened the conversation like grey mercury in the corners of his smile. You can't sweat every little thing.

The bill arrived without our asking for it: the kitchen had closed and we were the last diners in the place. We stood up unsteadily. Lars insisted on paying, fumbling with platinum credit cards. The waiters had cleared our table before we left the room.

Chapter 13

So Candy had gone and Jules had no closer friend and he was my responsibility now. The doctors made it clear that it was a medical decision and that legally they didn't require my permission, but I had asked to see them anyway and they had agreed to it, reluctantly. I was an unshaven, red-eyed formality. They probably thought I was causing trouble but I didn't care – I wanted to be there. It wasn't right that Jules was in the hands of total strangers. The street signs directing traffic to the hospital were the same as before: a single arrow and a word. I parked out back and flipped down the glove-box lid and did a big, fat line: as much as I could handle.

Hayden was waiting for me in her office with the clinical director, Dr Sauer, a short-haired man wearing a suit and a finger stall. We talked about the power cuts while we waited for the general manager, who arrived five minutes late, apologising. She was wearing a gold-coloured bracelet and a nervous flush.

'Thank you for coming in, Mr Usher,' she said. 'Can I begin by saying how sorry management was to learn about this situation. It must be stressful for you. Josephine', she nodded at Hayden, 'has asked

Philip and myself to be part of today's meeting. There are a lot of technical details to go through – I work here every day and still find it confusing.' She smiled. 'But I'm sure we'll find our way through it all. We know how stressful this can be.'

Sauer clasped his hands. 'We've been monitoring the patient,' he said. 'Dr Hayden and I have made separate examinations and there is no variation in the data. All signs are consistent with a person who is no longer alive. We believe that continuing mechanical support would be asking a person to remain beyond their time. If a patient is not going to recover, we would be visiting an indignity upon their person.'

He looked at the wrapping around his finger and then at me.

'As I said, we monitor patients and, in some cases, see signs that give cause for optimism. We don't see those signs here. And we have been looking closely. We have the same hopes as you do. I hope this doesn't sound cold or unfair.'

I wiped my nose with the back of my hand. It was stuffy in the room. The manager leaned forward.

'Samuel,' she said, 'as you know, management and staff have made every commitment to achieving a positive outcome. I think you can see that we have passed several milestones. What Dr Hayden and Dr Sauer are saying is that, as part of our expertise, we have to look ahead. We're asking you to work with us in reviewing the situation and committing to the best way forward.'

They had such a sophisticated way of saying nothing could be done, three people shrugging in slow motion. It wasn't about releasing Jules. It was about releasing them. Even with all their authority they still wanted to be told they were doing the right thing.

As I left Dr Hayden gave me a look that I recognised: not remote or unfeeling but efficient, the face of someone who had run out of time to listen, who could make a decision about life and death as quickly as an elevator running between floors.

In the corridor stood a man with two children, his hands resting on their soft blond heads. The little girl had a red cardigan and a wand. The boy was holding a jet plane. The place smelled of food that had been boiling for too long.

There was no grass behind the hospital buildings themselves, only cement and the roar of furnace stacks behind the car park. The parking lines were painted with yellow numbers. The dumpster was choked with hamburger wrappers and paper soft-drink cups, the generic trash issued to all premises in the city. Constable Howard and his plain-clothes partner were standing beside it with their hands in their pockets, waiting. I stared as they introduced themselves.

Howard didn't suit his uniform. He was too young and too short for the bright blue nylon jacket. He looked like it was itching him. The detective, Tangiers, was wearing a tapa-pattern short-sleeved shirt. He was chewing gum and there were acne scars under his three-day beard. He acted more like a shadow than a partner, listening to the younger cop without comment. When I gave Howard the letter Tangiers leaned over his shoulder to read it.

'These are all numbers?' Howard said. He sounded like more of a fool than he had to be.

'That's right,' I said. 'They're just numbers, as far as I can tell.'

'Do you know if they mean anything?'

'I don't know. I don't think so.'

'And he mailed them to you? Do you have the envelope?'

I showed it to him.

'What's ITD?' Howard said, reading the address.

'It's where I work.'

'What do you do there?'

'Reconstruct data.'

He looked up. 'You decode stuff?'

'Not really. It's just a job.'

'So he could have been sending you this to decode.'

'He didn't say why he sent it to me.'

'You spoke with him,' Tangiers said. 'When was that?'

'He called me, a little while ago. I wonder if this was why.'

'What did you talk about?'

'I don't know. It's a good question, though.'

'He's a scientist or something, your friend?' Howard said.

'He lectured at the university. I think it might be a page of his notes or something.' I shrugged. 'Have a look for yourself.'

'Are these phone numbers or something?' Howard said.

'They don't look like phone numbers.'

'What do these words mean? Anyway, goodbye. Like a suicide note.'

'He didn't commit suicide – unless he beat himself up,' I said.

'Sorry,' Howard said. 'We have to ask.'

'No, you don't.'

'What else was your friend dealing with?' Tangiers said.

'I said, he worked at the university.'

'You know what I mean.'

He was watching me. My hands were shaking and I was sniffing audibly.

'I honestly don't know,' I said.

'How long have you known him?' Tangiers said.

I thought about it. 'I guess it's not that long,' I said.

'So, he was more of an acquaintance. He wasn't really your good friend.'

'So do you know what happened to him?' I said.

'We think he was mugged. Maybe a drug transaction.'

'For a minute we thought he'd drowned,' Howard said. Tangiers shot him a look.

'Drowned?' I said. 'He was found in the city, on the street.'

'He was soaking wet. Head to toe,' Howard said.

'That could have happened afterwards,' Tangiers said. 'It wasn't clear how he got that way. It's possible it rained.'

'It hasn't rained in weeks,' I said.

'Did he like to swim?' Howard said, helplessly.

'Wearing his clothes?'

Howard flicked through his notebook as if it might contain a better answer.

'We'd like to talk to you again at some point,' Tangiers said. He put the letter back in its envelope. 'Do you mind if I take this?'

'Go ahead.' I had made a copy. I was being as cooperative as possible. He looked me in the eye.

'Watch yourself, mate,' he said. 'There's some bad shit doing the rounds.'

Deep in the building, it would be over soon. People were acting as if it had been meant to happen, and maybe it was. Jules knew what he was doing. We all did. Police and doctors dedicate themselves to saying careful, slow down, stop, but nobody listens. All of it: warnings on cigarette packets, crash helmets, stop lights, shark nets – everything. Don't do this or that. Nobody pays attention. These aren't warnings. They're signposts people miss while they're speeding past.

Fears are wishes. People want bad things to happen. It's why they talk about them all the time, in newspapers, on TV. Crashing is all people think about. They want to go faster. They want to lose control and spin out and OD. They want to fuck up. The only thing they're scared of is the wait.

Howard and Tangiers sat talking in their unmarked saloon and I sat in my car waiting for them to piss off. It took a good ten minutes for them to finish whatever they were yakking about and drive around the corner. I waited another minute to make sure they were gone and then flipped down the glove-box lid.

Chapter 14

The light was fading as I drove back to town. The power was still on in a lot of places, flickering like a fire burning to the embers without ever really being extinguished. Entire streets were shutting down now, changing the shape of the city.

I wanted to go somewhere where nobody knew me so I checked into a manga room in Elliot Street, a narrow one-way lane lined with Asian restaurants and bars. I paid the cover charge and took my complimentary Kirin and sat down. The young men around me were hunched over the latest comics, talking in hushed voices, ignoring their warming glasses of beer and the skipping beats of Japanese pop songs. The bare brick walls were decorated with posters of soft-porn cartoon girls and kendo swordsmen. The trestle tables were set with dainty napkins. The fish in the chiller glowed an evil green.

I stayed there for a couple of hours, getting up only to buy another drink or use the men's room. The bathrooms smelled like dry bread but the toilets were clean and the cistern lids were new and smooth, without chips or scratch marks.

I left around midnight. When I got outside I couldn't reach my car. A tow-truck had blocked the street trying to move a van. People were standing around watching the operator reverse, inch forward and reverse again. It was a warm night and he was putting on a good show. I left him to it and walked up the hill.

Most places were open. The casino had hired army equipment to keep the one-armed bandits and neon signs flashing twenty-four hours a day. Sunset had come and everyone had just kept going.

The Normandy was wired. They had put bouncers on the door. When I arrived some guy was being given a tap for throwing up in the toilets. Nearby two guys in suits and ties were picking a fight. The bouncers wouldn't let me in. I explained that I was a member but they still said no.

I went walking along K Road. The women on the corners were pacing in short skirts, unfolding their arms when a passing car slowed, blowing cigarette smoke as they asked the drivers for a light.

Sirens whistled up ahead. A Holden was suspended in the middle of the sidewalk, its wheels a foot off the ground. The marks on the pavement showed where it had taken the corner at speed, skidded and driven up on a line of pedestrian bollards. The chassis was wedged tight on the barrier but the engine was still running, sending up puffs of blue exhaust. The driver was nowhere to be seen. A cop was trying to cut the engine without pushing the car over.

More police cars were pulling up, cordoning off the scene of the accident. The prostitutes had abandoned their patches down the road and were moving softly between the men in the crowd, stopping them to ask for the time. They materialised, made eye contact, turned a blank expression into enquiry. A blonde in a plastic jacket took one guy's arm and they slipped away. As I watched them leave the others stared back, eyes shining like cats in a driveway.

The cop gingerly opened the Holden's door and got the key and twisted it slowly out of the ignition but the engine didn't stop.

'Why's it doing that?'

I jumped. The girl who had spoken was standing right beside me. She touched my arm. She was Thai, maybe, her red punk shock pushed back by a band. She was wearing blue crystal ear-rings shaped like teardrops and an orange fake fur coat.

'Why's it still going?' she said again. 'He took the keys out.'

'The engine's dirty,' I said. 'It's running on the little bit of gas inside.'

'But he's taken the key out.' The blue glitter on her eyelids made her gaze metallic. She was stoned and sparkling with low, wide eyes. 'Why doesn't the engine stop?' she said.

'I don't know.'

Her pale lipstick smiled.

'Are you okay, darling?' she said. 'You look so tired.'

She had put her arm through mine and was already leaning against me. Her platform sandals made us eye to eye. Her toenails were painted the same blue as her ear-rings.

'I live just near here,' she said. 'Do you want to come to my place?'

'Sure.'

'You've got money, haven't you, darling?'

'Yes.'

'That's a good thing. Do you want one of my girlfriends to join us?'

'No. Just you.'

'That's a good thing,' she smiled.

'We need to get a taxi,' I said, but she was already hailing one, nodding as I talked like this was a conversation she had all the time.

Her hands were warm and moist and the bangles around her wrists rattled with each quick step. She straightened my lapels.

'This is such a beautiful jacket. Where'd you get it? Very handsome.' She pressed the front panels flat with her hand.

'My name's Lucy,' she added, as if it was about to slip her mind.

The taxi stand was under a line of dead billboards. Lucy pointed at one that showed a woman's giant hand holding a champagne glass in front of holiday islands.

'That's me,' Lucy said. 'See? That's my hand. I'm a model.'

We got into a taxi and the driver pulled out and turned down a dark street, away from the crowds gathering around the stranded Holden. We drove past a record store. There was a poster of a woman's legs in the window.

'That's me as well,' she said. 'I do legs, backs, hands. There are bits of me all around here.'

'But not your face?'

'No, silly. Too Asian.'

The taxi stopped outside a cylindrical apartment tower that was mostly dark except for security lights and candle flames. I held up some notes. The driver picked them out like cards from a deck.

Lucy led me into the basement. The elevator doors were wedged open with a chair. The lift button panel was covered in a confusion of plastic and handwritten numbers and none of them worked. Lucy said she was in apartment 15, which was button 7B – the ninth floor. We took the fire stairs. I was walking so crooked she had to wait on each floor for me to catch up.

The landing on the ninth was bathed in moon-light. The air-conditioning wasn't working. There was no muffled spill from stereos or TVs – and no traffic sound. There was a rubber plant standing outside the elevator and its leaves were flashing red. The lift was frozen but the red arrows were blinking on and off, up and down.

Lucy took out her keys and opened the door and led me into a lounge lit with candles. The room looked white but I couldn't be sure. The only furniture inside it was a leather sofa and a ghetto blaster and some little plants on a glass coffee table.

Magazines and CDs were stacked on the floor. A tie-dyed scarf was pinned on the wall. The big windows opened on to a tiny balcony surrounded by blacked-out buildings.

'You want something to drink, honey?'

Lucy dumped her bag on the kitchen bench and opened the refrigerator. The light didn't come on. She popped the tabs on two cans of soft drink and handed one to me. I stared at the tiny bottles propped in the egg rack.

'Nail polish,' she said. 'If you leave it out it goes lumpy.'

I touched the unit. It felt cool and then very hot, and then cool again. I put the can down. I was having cold sweats. I had started to shake.

'Are you all right, honey?' she said. 'You look a bit rough.'

'I'm just coming down.'

'Oh, don't come down, baby. Not now.'

I walked back into the lounge but didn't make it to the sofa. My legs gave out. I had to lie out flat on the floor. It felt soft.

'Oh baby,' Lucy said, crouching down next to me. 'You need to take something. Do you want to see what I can find?' She reached for her purse. 'You don't have to leave. You can stay right here.'

My arms and legs felt like they had been dug into sand.

'Baby? Stay calm.' She was digging into the bag. 'Breathe. You're having palpitations.' She brought out a phial and pressed it under my nose. 'Suck it back.'

I snorted. The rush hit fast. The room swelled up like a balloon.

'The trick's to keep breathing,' she said, stroking my forehead. 'You're cool.'

She kissed my cheek. Her breath smelled of gas-station perfume and cigarettes.

'It's just sleep catching up,' she said.

I didn't want to sleep. There was too much travelling through my veins, not all of it chemical. She kept talking to me as I lay there. I watched her lips without hearing her. She popped the phial under my nose again. She pushed it up her own nostril and snorted and her eyes rolled back, pushing tears down the sides of her cheeks.

Breathe, she said.

Breathing through a machine like a pneumatic doll, armless and blind. Drinking air through a clear plastic tube, the throat checked for obstructions. The patient on a ventilator may have swallowed objects, may have vomited, puke stringing on to the sheets as a crowd in white coats gathers around the bed.

She shrugged off the orange fur coat. A snake tattoo was crawling around her shoulder. I ran my finger down it.

'You like that?' she said.

I tried to say that I did.

She pressed her mouth against my ear, moved her tongue, licked her teeth.

One thousand and one, one thousand and two.

Tip the head to one side, listen for the exhalation. Check that the lips and eyelids are not blue. Repeat the process until the patient responds.

'Is this a nice rush, baby?'

The tide was washing over Lucy. Lucy was turning very warm and very happy. She tipped back my head. She licked my neck. She marked me with an X.

Chapter 15

I walked back to my car the next morning and drove home. The rush hour was lighter than usual but the simple rule about work was that I would be running late no matter what time it was. I parked outside my building and went inside.

When I got to the top of the stairs I found two strangers standing by my door. They were in their twenties and dressed like businessmen in shirts and ties. The kid with the bleached hair was carrying copies of a magazine and the one with the shaved head was holding a plastic carry bag.

'How did you get in?' I said.

'The door was open,' the bleached kid said.

It was true. The power had gone off in the building and the security locks were down. I remembered seeing two bikes on the street.

'Selling isn't permitted in the building,' I said.

'We're talking to everyone,' the bleached kid said.

'We thought you might be interested in a subscription,' said his friend.

They watched me as I put my key in the lock. They looked nervous but I couldn't figure why.

'I mean it,' I said. 'You have to leave.'

They moved towards the stairs. I went inside my

apartment and latched the door and looked through the peephole. They were still standing outside, looking at each other. I called out and they moved down the stairs.

I didn't like the building being open like this. I called the supervisor. He took it the wrong way. I was shouting because of the situation, not because of him. I hung up. I checked the hall again. They seemed to have left.

My clothes smelled of cigarettes. My throat was hoarse and my nostrils were raked pink. There was no hot water and I couldn't make coffee. I ran a glass of water from the tap. It tasted warm. The food in the freezer was soft to touch and a layer of cool grey water had gathered around it in the tray.

The power was still on at work but I had to get Holly to buzz me in. My swipe card was missing along with all the cash from my wallet. Lucy had stolen them while I was passed out on the floor.

Raymond had made a little barricade of empty Fanta bottles along the front of his longboard. An uneven beard dusted his soft cheeks and his sneakers and socks had been thrown into the corner of the office. He was rocking back in his chair, bending a foil aspirin packet back and forth along the perforated line. The lights on his phone were flashing, help-lessly.

'Can you believe it?' he said. 'There was another major outage at three this morning. The CBD went down for an hour. They're calling it a minor interruption. They're telling people to carry on like normal and the whole grid is failing. It's all just gonna blow.'

'There's no security in my building,' I said. 'I caught Jehovah's Witnesses walking around.'

'You look like shit.'

'Holly just told me.'

'Is it that hospital thing?'

I nodded. I showed him the copy I had made of the letter. 'Can you make anything of this?'

'Which job is it?'

'It's something I found. It's probably just numbers.'

'All this is just numbers,' he said, waving the letter at the office. 'All data is numbers. The power cuts, the economy, the whole Western world, everything. Other civilisations built pyramids and religions: we just do numbers. Vectors on a building plan. Personal identification numbers. Missile launch codes – it's all the same. The end of the world is just numbers.'

He popped an aspirin out of the packet and chewed it dry.

'Just tuck it into the back of your head that this could be way more important than what it looks like, is all I'm saying.'

'Sure,' I said.

'Just trying to cheer you up, big guy.'

'So how do I find out what they mean?'

'Normally I'd get my best man on to it, but you're my best man and look at you.' Bits of crushed white pill were sticking to his tongue. 'You look like your heart's gonna jump out of your chest.'

'I'm fine, really.'

'You're doing way too much shit, Sam. It's not a race. It'll catch up, mate. Karma and everything.'

'I'm keeping it together.'

'Are you paranoid yet? Seeing things? You should sleep. No drugs, no piss. Clean the toxins out of your system. Are you eating?'

'I'm doing fine, Ray.'

'Yeah, I know. Everything's turning to shit.'

I watched Raymond as he lapsed into silence again to read the letter. He was a dumb kid who thought he was infallible. But he was right about the heart thing. It felt like I'd swallowed something that was still alive.

'Anyway and goodbye,' he said. 'This is encrypted?'

'Why do you say that?'

'Anyway has six letters and goodbye has seven letters . . . It could be a cryptogram key.'

'Who works with cryptograms around here?'

'Lotsa people. I can think of two firms, locally.' He held up two fingers to show me how many two was. 'New Zealand sells software to the military and to people who, you know, are doing naughty things. That could be what this is.' He shrugged. 'Have you tried dialling them?'

'What?'

'Have you dialled the words on a phone?'

I took out my phone and tried different combinations of prefixes and letters. *Goodbye* wasn't a number. *Anyway* rang. A woman answered.

'Hello?' she said.

'Hi,' I said.

'Who's calling?'

'I wondered if we could meet up.'

'Have I seen you before?'

'No. My name's Sam.'

'Go to the carnival,' she said, and hung up.

Raymond had started bending the next section of the foil packet.

'Is there a carnival on in town?' I said.

'There's a club called Carnival.'

'Can you tell me where it is?'

'Sure thing.' Raymond grinned. 'This is why I'm way richer than you, matey.'

The Carnival was down a stairwell at the end of a bright arcade. The music pounding beneath the floor tiles was a reminder that it was still night in another part of the world. Instead of a sign there was a piece of paper on the door that read We have POWER!!!! and a smiling bouncer. I paid him my twenty dollars and he let me straight in, and then I tripped and fell over.

I landed on my hands and knees. I had been outside driving through bright sunlight and the club was pitch black. The floor was split level, like a Californian mansion, and I had walked straight off the edge. Falling and picking myself up attracted no attention. The people inside the room were dancing. A few were crawling around themselves.

Gradually my eyes adjusted. There was a cigarette machine with a dying fern and two teenagers standing beside it. Beyond the different colours of the dance floor was a line of old lounge furniture and a pinball game nobody was playing. Kids slouched in the couches and chairs. The boys had grins and the girls had big ear-rings. There were dreadlocked white boys and girls in camouflage and goth couples in fur and skinheads and punks and disco kids, all beamed down from fifty years' worth of the same dumb chords mashed ten different ways, all nodding to reggae's dull consensus, dipping their pretty heads on the three beat.

I didn't begrudge their having a good time. I sat up at the bar feeling older than I was. But I had come this far and I could wait to find out what Jules had sent me. There was a blonde girl dancing in the crowd. She wasn't Candy.

The barman had a skinny neck and bumpy pimples on his forehead and long tattoos poking out from his T-shirt sleeves. He was smoking a rollie and tapping his foot to the music. I waited for him to come over and serve me. When he did, I introduced myself.

'I'm a friend of Candy and Jules,' I said.

'Candy and Jewels?'

'You don't know them?'

He didn't have a clue what I was talking about. I ordered a beer and he spent a full minute looking through the chiller. When he brought it over I held out the money and he stared at it while he scratched his stomach.

'What's wrong?' I said.

'New tat.' He lifted his shirt to show me the flaming dice and the skull running around his rib cage. It was covered in some sort of sterile plastic wrap. 'Robert Williams, you know it?'

'Who did it?'

'Guy up on College Hill. They're still the best. They get the best colour. They mix detergent with the dyes to get the shades. But this is the last one.'

'You have others?'

He showed me the Hokusai on his back. 'I don't get the rush any more,' he said. 'Now it just hurts and shit, especially around my ribs. You know? Your body gets tired after a while. You got any?'

I scratched my shoulder. I shook my head.

More people were arriving. A different DJ came on. The dub segued into something faster and people starting getting up and going back on the dance floor. Something else was kicking in: energy, chemicals, you could feel it. They were all caught in the wave.

'I thought you'd be shut,' I said.

'Not us,' he said. 'You hear the mayor on the radio? He's telling everyone to stay out of town, like he's Wyatt Earp or something. He's killing the city. I know places that have gone broke already. This is the summer season. This is when people make money for the whole year.'

'So how long has this been going?'

'Two days.'

'Bullshit. Really?'

He nodded. 'Pretty staunch.'

'A friend gave me the number here,' I said. 'Well, not the number – the word. The alphanumeric.'

'How's that?'

'Anyway. Like when you dial a–n–y–w–a–y on the phone.'

'Oh right.' Now he understood. 'You're waiting for Helen.'

'Helen.'

'Helen Anyway.'

'That's right.' Now I was the one catching on. 'I'm waiting for Helen Anyway. Is she around?'

'Don't know. You can't rush her. A lot of people want to rush. It happens when it happens.'

'How much?'

He shrugged. 'Wouldn't know, mate.'

There was a cash terminal beside the till. I asked him what the limit was and he told me. I withdrew the full amount and he laid it out on the bar. I left it there.

I had another beer and made a phone call, shouting over the dub. As I hung up he came back and asked me where I was headed after this and I said the Freyburg Hotel.

'I'll be there tonight,' I said. 'So if you see Helen –'

'I'll tell her.'

'It's an old place. You want the number?'

'No worries.'

'You sure you'll remember?'

'I'll remember.'

'So will she call?'

'I'll tell her.'

I left.

Outside, workers had ripped up a big section of road. The traffic was being diverted so the power company could fix the cables, the cars crawling bumper to bumper in an angry loop. At the intersection one driver lost his patience and tried to break out, driving up on to the sidewalk only to be blocked again. Someone leaned on the horn. Pedestrians swore. The driver got out and started yelling back. The workers just kept digging.

Chapter 16

The Freyburg was a grey hotel down by the wharves, one of the oldest in the city. Two yellow generator trucks were parked outside, black cables snaking between them. A lot of people around the city were checking into hotels because their apartments had no power. The gilt-edged mirrors in the foyer multiplied the crowd: tourists armed with video cameras and windbreakers, locals in rumpled street clothes. There was muzak playing and the doormen wore long coats and the forecourt smelled of truck diesel and salt coming off the sea.

The concierge had dyed hair and a lisp that made him pronounce my name as Other. He asked if I was taking a holiday. I was, but not from much.

'Will you be dining?' he said. 'Will there be luggage?

'No, just me.'

'You may be aware of the power problem. In your room you will find a letter containing information in the event of that occurring. We hope you enjoy the Freyburg, Mr Other. Have a good evening.'

The same muzak was playing in the elevator. There were more mirrors on the walls. I swiped the room card and stood as my reflections rose, repeating and shrinking like ripples in a pool.

The room was on the eleventh floor. The corridor was a regimental parade of muted doors and up-lighting. The walls were dark blue trimmed with brushed aluminium. The doors were fitted with spy holes and locks that opened with a card. The room was white and smelled like new carpet. There were two beds and a desk and chair by the window.

I put my phone on the nightstand. I went through the drawers, the corners of the room. I looked under the beds. I don't know what I was looking for, but I thought someone might be watching. I picked up the phone and listened. The dial tone sounded normal. I called up room service and ordered two bottles of champagne. When they arrived I pretended to be in the shower while the boy brought it in. Enough people had seen me check in downstairs. I signed the chit through the door and sat on the toilet lid while he stood the bucket by the bed. The vanity was cardboard-coloured marble. I looked pale in the mirror.

When he finally left I opened the first bottle and sat by the window. The falling sun turned the city orange. People were moving gently through the streets. This is what it would look like if a nuclear pulse hit: planes hanging in the sky, machines stopped, everything frozen. It felt like someone had dropped a slow bomb.

She called me to come down and meet her.

'It's Helen,' she said. 'I'm in the lobby.'

I took the elevator. She was standing with her back to the doors when they opened. She kept her face turned away as she stepped in so we could check each other out in the reflections. She was small, with long, black hair. She was wearing a caramel leather pants suit and carrying a fringed suede satchel and a coloured sports bag with something heavy inside. She dropped the sports bag between her battered high heels. Her pale hands were as fine as a child's and her fingernails were painted green. I thought she was pretty until she smiled.

At the room I opened the door but she motioned me to go first, checking the hallway before she stepped inside. She checked inside the bathroom as she passed it and peeked between the blinds, smiling at me all the time. She lifted the sports bag on to the table and stood holding the satchel.

'So,' she said. 'How's it going?'

'Fine.'

'That's really cool.' She smiled again. 'So what have you been up to this evening?'

'Not a lot.'

'Yeah? Do you like music?'

'Sure.'

'I brought my deck.' She unzipped the sports bag and peeled it off a ghetto blaster and a folder of CDs. 'Do you like *Low*? "Speed of Life" is my favourite. I listen to it over and over. Is that champagne?'

I poured her a glass while she put the track on. Metallic chiming filled the room. She sat on the single chair and crossed her legs. She opened a gilt purse and took out a cigarette.

'This is a smoking room, huh?' she said.

'No.'

'Cool.' She lit the cigarette. 'I haven't seen you before, have I?'

'No.'

'Blondie said you were okay.'

'The barman? What makes him Blondie?'

'All he does is take messages.'

'So why are you Helen Anyway?'

'Excuse me?'

'Your name?'

She rolled her eyes like the question bored her. 'Someone worked out that if you call my number, the letters on the phone spell out Anyway.'

'The person who worked that out, was his name Jules?'

She sipped the champagne. 'No.'

'Tall guy.' I described his face and clothes. 'Mathematician. I think he knew you.'

'Oh. The Professor. He gave you my number?'

'He wrote to me.' I took out the letter and showed her. 'See there?'

Something in her face moved before she had time to shake her head. 'What's that?'

'It's the letter he wrote me. And see, there's your name.'

'It's just a word.'

'It's your name – the number I dialled.'

'It's just the same word.'

'Everybody has a nickname?'

'Sure.'

'What's mine?'

'So far, you're nobody.'

She flicked ash on the carpet. The letter was putting her off so I slipped it back in my pocket.

'Jules did give me your number, though,' I said.

'Cool. Whatever. So we're here.'

'We're good friends,' I said. 'We like the same things. That's why I called.'

'Well, Blondie fixed me up, so we're sweet.'

I refilled her glass. She took a phial of white crystals out of her satchel and tapped out two white lines. 'You're all nervy,' she said. 'This'll bring you down.'

It had no taste and stuck in my nostrils. I coughed.

'It's good for you,' she said. 'Drink some more and have the rest.'

'You finish it.'

'No baby, it's for you. On the house.'

We sat on the bed but she was still playing it cool. She started making small talk about the city and the blackouts. I tried to get her to talk about Jules. She was good at avoiding the subject. I started asking her again and then stopped in mid-sentence as my face went numb and my ears filled with wax and the bed covers between my fingers turned to grease. She smiled when she saw it hit. It had only taken a few minutes.

'How do you feel now?' she said. 'Are you relaxing now? Is it coming on? Are your hands warm?' She giggled. 'Don't try to talk. You want another bump?'

'You have some.'

'I started early. This is for you, baby. I want you to get ready.'

The music changed to slow jet engines and Japanese strings. She cut more lines on the table. I did them and fell back on the bed. She unbuttoned my shirt. She touched my shoulder.

'What happened to you?' she said. 'That must have hurt terribly. How does it feel now?'

'It feels fine.'

She tapped something else into the gap between the tendons of her thumb. She cupped her hand under my nose.

'Let yourself go,' she said. 'Turn on.'

I sucked hard. I wanted to trash everything I had known. Everyone was gone now and I was the last one left. I was sobbing on their behalf. She tapped out more for herself. Her face became mine. I was crying because I was her, because she was tired and alone.

'Don't you love this song?' she said. 'I just love this song.'

She took off her jacket. Beneath the leather her skin looked like vinyl. Her shoulder was tattooed with a snake. I touched it. I asked what it was.

'This is Midgard,' she said. 'At the end of the world the snake swallows the sun. You like that story? It's a legend, like an ancient legend. I knew this guy – he was telling me the legend and I wrote it down and I promised myself I would keep it, you know, like for ever.'

The sweat was running down my temples. I tried to keep talking but I couldn't. My mouth was filling with saliva. My body was melting. I let it melt. She snapped off the lights.

'How are you going there, honey?'

The question bobbed like a spirit. I felt for her words. She took hold of my wrists and my arms got longer. Her fingers took my hair and pulled back my head. I rolled in the sheets, travelling through the layers of murk and despair, elation and exhaustion.

'Breathe,' she said. 'The trick's to keep breathing.'

The bed was warmer than my bed. Warmer and softer and better. She whispered in my ear.

'I've got something for the Professor,' she said. 'Would you like that?'

'What is it?'

'You said you were friends.'

'Yes.'

'You said you like the same things. Don't you want it? It's got his name on it. You just stay there and relax and lose all that tension. I'm just going to get ready, okay?'

'What happens with this shit? Does it zoom? Is there a zoom coming?'

'Big fucking zoom, honey. Just you wait.'

She picked up the suede bag and went to the bathroom.

And then the distance between my temples collapsed, negative-universe style, until my head was no thicker than my wrist. I could hear water drumming. My chest was warm. I was in falling lava. My fingers stretched out from the stream into dark space, past the blue stratosphere. If you lift your arms you fly like a satellite, sucking up noise. The steam is smoke flavoured with nothing and the floor is a map gridded like a landscape.

I worked my jaw.

The pool of water outside the house widens like a flask. The water is grey and cool, mangrove roots poking up like antennae. But there are no mosquitoes, and the mud weighs no heavier on a footstep than a bed sheet. Every stride trails streaks of silt through the glacé. A paddle steamer lies on its side in the pool, the hull exposed from bow to stern. The deck railings are within reach. The green paint has been kept clean by the rain. The metal is cold. You balance carefully as you step aboard. The water is still. Sand makes a causeway out to the boat, the passengers' escape when it mired. Something pale is gliding through the water but it will not venture into the shallows. Something flat with white, pointed teeth.

I don't know when I woke up. It was pitch black. The air was still. The air-conditioning wasn't working. I rolled off the bed. The floor was wet. I crawled to the curtains and pushed them open. It was dark outside also, and straight away, fucked as I was, I realised what had happened. The whole grid had gone down.

The city was blacked out.

I tried to stand up. The carpet squelched. The whole floor was soaked. There was a rushing noise. I turned my head to check but it wasn't a hallucination. I could hear water running.

I called Helen's name. She didn't answer.

Outside in the hall, people were barking instructions. I felt my way along the wall. My breathing was loud. The journey of a few feet seemed to take hours. The water was running out of the bathroom. I couldn't open the door. I knocked and called out.

Suddenly there was a bright flash inside the room. The generator trucks had kicked in and brought on the lights. I shut my eyes. I was standing in water: the current would run me through like a skewer. I let go of the wall but the bedside lights were already shorting out, blinking and popping, and then the room fell dark again. Outside, the lights in the hall stayed on. The water gleamed as it crept under the door.

I tested the handle. I tried the bathroom door but it wouldn't move. I put my shoulder against it and pressed hard and it opened. A tiny wave of red water washed out, running gently across my feet, and then Helen Anyway slithered out and wedged in the opening. Her lips were blue and her mouth was filled with spit. Her eyes were rolled back. The strap of her bag was tied around the snake and the hypodermic was stuck in its head.

Chapter 17

I shut my eyes and opened them again but she was still there. She looked like a blue photograph of the woman who had entered the room, her bloody hair spread out like a halo on the cold bathroom tiles. I stared in stoned amazement. She didn't move. The veins in her neck were blue. Her wrist was cold. I touched her throat, feeling for her pulse like I was fumbling for a lost set of keys. There was no movement. It was too late. There was nothing I could do.

I stepped over her and turned off the taps. The mirror was splattered with bile. Her satchel was blocking the overflow drain. I pulled it out. The wet suede was black and heavy. The blood-reddened water started pouring down the grate.

I dropped the satchel and the water inside it spilled out, puking the contents across the floor. A tiny gun fell out. At first I thought it was a toy or a novelty lighter but then I picked it up and felt the weight and realised it was real. It was a black and silver snub-nose, what kids call a baby nine, and it fitted in my palm. The safety was on.

Her phone was in the bag. I took it: it was carrying a record of my call. There were bottles of pills and zip-lock baggies filled with crystals and powders. I started putting them in my pockets. I had a vague idea about getting rid of anything suspicious she was carrying. I stumbled back into the room holding the gun. What sort of person was she expecting to meet?

I put it in my pocket. I picked up my things. I could feel something hard behind my eyes, pushing. I was seeing lights spinning three different ways. I needed to get out and get my story straight. I checked the spy hole. The corridor was an empty goldfish bowl. I stepped out and closed the door behind me. The fire escape was open. I went downstairs.

Outside the Freyburg the guests were following the fire-drill procedure, assembling in groups in front of the building. Lots of people were wet: the sprinklers had come on, and it was dark. I blended right in. I slipped through the crowd.

When I got into my car I opened one of the baggies and dumped it across the dashboard and snorted it and scooped up the remainder in my fingertips, rubbing it around my teeth. Everything was swirling. I had to sharpen up.

The city was black. I watched the road markings, chanting nonsense. All I had to do was follow the car in front. Handling the wheel was like trying to balance a ball. I had a baby nine and a dead woman's drugs in my pockets.

My phone rang.

'Mr Other?' It was the concierge. 'We're outside your room. Can you come to the door?'

'Just a minute.'

'We're going through the floor. We're evacuating the hotel, Mr Other. Could you come to the door?'

'I'll be out in a second. I'll meet you downstairs.'

'It would be good if you could open the door now.'

The lane was slowing. I tried to turn and another driver hit the horn.

'Mr Other? Are you in there?'

I heard him telling someone to open it. I hung up. I was fucked. They would already be stepping on the wet carpet, looking down at the blood, the blue corpse. I needed to get as far away as I could to think. Up ahead, a curve cut into the harbour waters like an obsidian blade: the bridge, its spotlights dead.

I was a fool to imagine I could reach it, let alone make it across, but I kept driving. I had lost all perception of time. It could have been hours since I left the hotel. My hands felt like they were in thick gloves. Sounds passed slowly as the road unfurled. The speedometer said ninety but nothing sudden occurred.

I was getting close to the bridge. I could smell my own sweat. There was pink face powder and blood on my clothes. It would only take a cop who was less than blind. I coasted towards the on-ramp, travelling either fast or slow. One of the two.

My phone rang again.

'This is Bill Howard, Sam. We met at the hospital. Do you mind telling me where you are now?'

'I'm not sure.'

'Are you in your car?' He quoted the model and registration.

'I'm just pulling into the hotel.'

'The Freyburg? Just now?'

'I'm in the forecourt.'

'I can't see you,' he said. 'Were you meeting someone in your room this evening, Sam? Because you see –'

I threw the phone out the window. He knew I was lying. They were looking for the car now: I couldn't drive further. A police helicopter was already coming towards me across the bridge, draping a fluorescent blanket across the lanes.

The road tilted up over the sea. Waves passed underneath me and cold air pushed through the window. I took the first turn off, steering in slow motion back towards the sugar factory.

The grounds were deserted. In the rear-view mirror, the city had disappeared. I coasted down the hill, past the trees. Cicada skins were stuck to the trunks and branches, amber ghosts split down their spines. I pulled up at the water's edge. My tongue was fat in my mouth.

I knew what I was doing. I had done it before. It wasn't going to hurt: I wasn't going to feel a thing and there would be no bad memories, nothing. All I would remember was the second before. There was nothing to fear as long as I did it fast, with no hesitation or thought for the future. The cold water would wake me up. Afterwards there would be only wreckage. As long as I didn't see that, nothing would have happened.

I opened the door. I held the clutch down and put the car in first. I pressed the accelerator and the engine sped. I released the accelerator and the noise fell back. The handbrake kept everything in place.

I pressed the pedal down and the engine went loud and then louder. I pressed hard and the engine raced. The steering was steady. I told myself I was in control.

At night when you swim you can't see the water but you know it's there. You remember where it is and you dive into your memory.

I started to bring up the clutch. Easing it in. And the whirring plates met and the car hugged the ground, digging itself in as the rear wheels started to turn. I kept the pedal down and the clutch midway, one hand on the wheel, the other on the brake. The wheels were spinning so fast the rear was beginning to fishtail. Dust and smoke clouded the headlights. I let the clutch out a little more and the car started to buck and the engine howled and it was hard to hold on now, very hard. And then, in one movement, I dropped the brake and let the clutch full out and the engine was released.

The car shot forward.

The edge of the road and the water and the bridge rushed up slowly. The car was a rocket, an atom smasher. The world accelerated and hollered and bumped and then there was no sound and the world was tipping forward and I was still pressed back in my seat and there was light suddenly and then none and a clap like nearby thunder and a satisfied hiss and then sleep.

When I woke up I was blind. I couldn't see anything. I started to fight with a different kind of fury and as I flailed something flashed in my eyes. My face was buried in something. Paper. A bag. The car's air bag had inflated and filled the compartment, blocking out the light. I clawed it away, panicking. The bag was enormous. Every time I pushed it down it popped out to fill another space. There was movement outside the windows. The headlamps were spiking through a green mist.

I was underwater. The darkness through the windows was the ocean.

My feet were cold, and getting colder. Water was soaking into my socks, the legs of my trousers. I ripped the bag out of its housing and pushed it aside. The foot compartment was full of water. The car was sinking. I pushed at the handle but the door wouldn't open. I would have to wait for it to fill and the pressure to equalise. Then I could swim calmly upwards, holding my breath and avoiding all entanglements, currents, big fish cruising the shore.

I knew what was happening but the fear rose with the water. I lost my nerve and reached for the window switch. The motor whined and shorted out and took the headlamps with it and I was in darkness again but the window had opened a few millimetres and water was spraying into the dry space like a shower. It ran around my belly. The sea was very close now.

Cold crept up my body. I didn't know how deep I was. Was the water around here deep or shallow? I had to wait. My chest felt tight. The cold water reached my mouth. I thrashed. I hit the door but couldn't open it. The locks had shorted out. The compartment was almost full. I was floating up to the roof, breathing the last gap of air. The baby nine was dragging my pocket down. I grabbed it and felt for the trigger and pressed it against the windscreen and fired. The flash lit up the green water and the windscreen disappeared and water poured in, stirring the gunpowder smoke.

I gasped and dived down and kicked through the shot-out window, swimming up with the gun in one hand. The water was like ice. After a few strokes my body was numb. I couldn't feel a thing. And then my head was hot and my hands were warm, the blood turning up its own dial.

I was drifting in the current past the jetty and the shallow bays and overhanging trees. As I floated past I saw Cleopatra's Needle on the bank. I didn't remember Cleopatra's Needle being there before but that didn't seem to matter now. I grabbed on to the steps and lay there for a time before I had the strength to haul myself up.

The monument was a silhouette in the darkness.

The sphinxes at its base were perfect and silent. I dropped between them and slumped against the bronze.

I was soaked to the skin. I checked my pockets, caught my breath. The stars were bright in the sky. The obelisk pointed up to them like a giant metronome hand frozen in the middle of a long, dark second.

Chapter 18

By sunrise the people chasing me would have tracked the car from the hotel to the refinery and reasoned that the body had been sucked out in the tide. It would spoil things if they found me sleeping a hundred yards away. I had to get started.

Traffic was moving across the harbour bridge. A taxi was not a good idea. Any driver would remember a fare soaked head to toe. The police would issue a broadcast to operators soon, if they hadn't already. I'd be radioed-in the moment I stepped out of the cab.

A stone path ran along the grass above the beach in sight of the houses along the shoreline. Walking was dizzy work but the other people getting twisted in the blackout would provide cover.

Yachts were moored across the inlet. The water was still. If I could get to a boat I could use it to cross, but the cabins would be padlocked. I didn't have the tools to break a lock. I didn't have the strength to swim out. The more I thought about it, the more the harbour looked like a moat.

I could hear laughter. There was a group of kids further along the beach: two girls and two boys. The girls were hunched together smoking, a bottle of

Jack Daniel's stuck between them in the sand. The boys were loading an aluminium dinghy that was slipping side to side in the breakers. They had seen me approach in my wet clothes: the laughter was at me.

The girls were wearing shoestring metallic disco tops and their bare arms were pale, barely thicker than the bone. The boy holding the dinghy was wearing camouflage army trousers soaked to the knee. The other boy was carrying two life-jackets and a slab. The weight of the beer made a dull thud as he dropped it in the metal hull. He said something to the first boy and walked back up the beach to a ute parked behind the grass and lifted out an outboard motor and a fuel can.

The boy holding the boat was the younger of the two and the most likely to listen. I tried to keep my balance as I walked up and asked him to take me across. The girls were still laughing but he was more nervous than amused. He looked at me like I was crazy. I fished out a bottle of pills. He looked in my palm, then at his mate, then at the girls. I shook out one and he took it over and they huddled around it, whispering. The girls stopped giggling.

I stood dripping water on the sand while the boys bolted on the engine. I insisted that only one of them take me across. They agreed. They could see I was no threat. The first boy held the boat so I could climb in. Pauly, his name was. The dinghy bobbed as he ripped the starter cord, and the engine kicked over. The onshore shimmered in blue smoke.

★   ★   ★

The shore disappeared as soon as we left it. The yachts slipped past in the mist. They were close enough to touch and as inviting as doorways. I wanted to board one and rest.

'That's her,' he said, pointing out a long sloop with a cream-yellow hull. 'The banana. We're just gonna hang out for the night. It's Mike's brother's boat – Mike's the guy back there.'

I nodded appreciatively – I couldn't say much.

'Looks like you've had quite a night. You been swimming or something?' He giggled. 'It's warm enough, aye. Good night for a swim. We were gonna stay in town but it's a pretty big hassle with the power cuts and shit.'

Pauly talked small. He wanted to keep his distance and stop me introducing anything he couldn't handle. I was too tired to think why. Although I couldn't see where we were headed I felt safe enough. Drugs were a solid trade.

The water was calm. Soft black waves drummed on the hull. We fanned a shallow wake as we crossed the middle of the harbour. A horn sounded from a big ship, shaking the thin aluminium dinghy.

'What's that?' I said.

'Freighter. We're probably in a shipping lane.'

'Is that safe?'

He shrugged. 'It's a working harbour. Lot of ships come through here, aye.'

I looked around. There were no lights approaching.

'We'll see them coming. They're pretty fucking big.'

I checked my pockets. I didn't want to swim again.

The city started to rise up. I could see the office buildings. A Morse code of rivet heads tracked the laced girders of the Eiffel Tower. I was getting my bearings now. I was near the Tower, or it was here, near me. I let my hand drift in the water, the phosphorescence dancing across my bloodied knuckles.

There are only two measures of time in the universe: what you know, and for ever. All you can prove is what you know.

I ran my tongue around the inside of my teeth.

'You feeling all right?' Pauly said.

'I think so.'

'Things getting kind of weird on you, huh? It's a pretty fucking out-of-it night. The whole place has just shut down.'

I was looking out for the Arc de Triomphe. Jules admired the way the roads radiated out from it. The police helicopters weren't flying over that part of the city. It was perfectly still.

I was pretty fucked up. I rubbed my forehead. The outboard motor shuddered and cut out. I looked up, startled. Pauly had tilted the screw up out of the water. He kept his hand on the ignition switch to demonstrate how he had flicked it.

'Whoops,' he said.

'What's wrong?'

'Motor's cut out, mate.' He glanced over his shoulder. 'We'll drift back to shore unless I can get it started again. Maybe you'd better get out. You reckon you can swim from here?'

'What do you mean?'

'I mean it doesn't look like we're going to make it. Maybe you should just swim. I mean, you really want to get across, right?'

'You said you'd take me across.'

'Yeah. How much did we say that would cost again? I can't remember.' He held out his hand. 'It's gotta be worth some more, aye. You know. For fuel and shit.'

It was impossible to tell in what direction the boat was pointed or the distance to shore. I took a breath and sat up. I started going through my pockets. Pauly grinned. I took out the gun and pointed it at him. He blinked.

'It's real,' I said.

He fiddled with the ignition. For a moment neither of us thought it was going to start. I could see the idea of being shot jumping around in his head. Finally the motor came back to life. Pauly dropped the propeller in the water and the bow kicked up and we started to move. I lowered the gun but kept it out where he could see it. The skyscrapers had disappeared behind a new mist or part of the night I hadn't seen before.

The marina was surrounded by a wave break: a low wall of split stones cemented together like sandbags. As we came up to it Pauly tillered the dinghy around and idled the motor. The boat drifted closer to the wall. When I could reach I grabbed it and climbed up.

Pauly clapped his hands, once.

'Hey,' he said. 'How about it? No hard feelings, mate.'

I threw him the bottle of pills. He caught it and put it in his jeans pocket. He engaged the motor again and swung back out in a shallow arc. I could hear the put-put of the motor a long minute after he disappeared.

I put the gun in my pocket and walked along the wall. The road around the marina led into the bottom of the city. Hundreds of boats were tied up at their moorings. The breeze was whipping the wire hawsers against the masts like thin applause.

Chapter 19

I rubbed my eyes. Blood was moving through my body again. I was thirsty now, and I would be hungry soon. I knew there was food and dry clothing in my apartment. There was a chance I could get there and slip inside to snatch what I needed before the police put a watch on the place.

The wet jacket pocket outlined the baby nine as perfectly as an X-ray. I took off my jacket and shook it out and used it to wrap Helen Anyway's things: the phone, the drugs, the gun. It was a warm night. The air would dry my shirt.

The fountains in the downtown square were switched off. The stars wobbled in their still waters.

As I walked between buildings I could see candles burning in a high room where the tenants were dining on the balcony. They were listening to crackling civil defence reports on the radio. Auckland was in a state of emergency. They changed the channel. They leaned over the railings to see who was walking below. I kept my head down.

Two men in suits got into a parked sports car and drove away honking the horn. I saw a group of kids hanging around the bus stop, smoking with their shirt hoods up, and crossed to avoid them. They were too young to cause real trouble but the fewer witnesses, the better.

A block later I came to a stop in front of a skyscraper. It was just another building but there was something strange about it. I knew it but I couldn't place the name. I walked up the steps and stared at the empty foyer inside. I waved at the glass doors but they didn't move. There was a security desk at the far end of the foyer with nobody behind it. The guards were probably out back. Maybe they were already on the phone. There were security cameras all around. I didn't want to be taped. I turned and started walking again but when I was a safe distance away I stopped and checked back. The spire reached up into the night like a hypodermic. I remembered its name, now. It was the Chrysler Building.

A street lamp flicked on as I approached, then off again after I passed.

It took a good hour to reach my street. My spirits lifted when I saw my building but as I walked closer a police car took shape, an unmarked late-model sedan with a whip antenna and the outlines of two officers inside. I was the only person out walking: they would notice if I stopped. I turned into the building before mine, walked up the unlit steps and pushed open the deactivated door. The apartments inside were locked. I kept walking through the foyer and out the fire escape doors at the rear, down the alley and back into the city in the direction I'd come from.

I had exited into nothing. I was tired from walking now, and no closer to food or drink. My clothes were still damp and the morning would only get colder before the sun came up. I thought about trading the drugs for cash. I touched my pocket. The photocopy of Jules' letter was still inside, folded into a tight wad. I unfolded it. The paper was delicate: the folds and outer edges were damp, but the centre was dry and it was still readable.

I walked to a phone booth and found the number of the Viscount. The house operator didn't want to wake Lars Dedit but I insisted. If Lars had been asleep he didn't sound like it.

'Sam. You are having a good time, I hope. You are all over the news. Fortunately most people's televisions are not working, so you are not so famous yet.'

'What does the news say?'

'That the whole power grid has failed, as you can see, and that the police are investigating the death of a woman in the Freyburg Hotel, a Miss Helen Arkusich. They are appealing to the public for more information, which I think is a sophisticated way of putting it. Has someone turned you in or are you dead?'

'Lars – I want to trade. I think I have something you want. Jules sent me a letter before he was attacked. He sent me a copy of his work.'

'Are you sure? You didn't tell me about it.'

'I heard you arguing in the museum. I wanted to

find out what was happening before I made the offer.'

'And now is a good time to sell.'

'I just need a little help and that's all.'

There was a pause as he checked his watch.

'I haven't done a deal with a dead man before,' he said. 'Where shall we meet?'

The city cemetery ran down a gentle hill, the plots saddling either side of Grafton Bridge. The moon cast soft, broken shadows between the trees. The headstones were some of the first dug in the city, thick tablets caked in moss. Even the vandalised tombs looked as if they had been snapped and jostled decades before.

In the centre was a stone mausoleum the size of a tool shed. The angel was chipped and the gate shuddered as it opened on its rusty hinges. I sat down inside and spread my jacket out. The gun was spotted with moisture but the bottles and baggies were still sealed. I brushed the marble clean with the soft flesh of my palm and laid out a long white line and snorted deep, rubbing the empty plastic on my gums. I chewed half a pill, choking on the bitterness. The shakes were subsiding when Lars appeared in his white suit, stepping between the headstones like a traveller searching for his seat on a foreign bus.

'Sam. The police were right – you did drown after all.' He was carrying a paper shopping bag with the hotel's name on it. 'I brought some food but, as you can imagine, there is not much open.'

The bag contained what was left of his hotel mini-bar: a box of chocolates and two bread rolls, a pat of butter wrapped in foil and a bottle of tonic water. It tasted good enough.

'The news item talked about narcotics,' Lars said. 'Nothing about a gun, however. Is it real?'

'It fires.'

'It's so small.'

I wiped my mouth. I took Jules' letter out of my pocket.

'I need money and I need clothes. And I need to get out of here. Can you do that?'

'Out of the country?' He nodded. 'My company sends couriers all the time. But you will need a passport, of course, and once you're overseas I can't help you. You'll have to make your own arrange-ments.'

'But you can do it?'

'Of course. It's simply a matter of making up papers. It doesn't even cost much – they do it all on computers now. It's easy to make you something that works once but I cannot guarantee you that you will get back in.'

'I'm not coming back. There's nothing here for me now – twice. How many guys can say that?'

He smiled.

I gave him the letter.

'Anyway,' Lars said. 'Freedom, goodbye.' He turned the page over, holding it up. He squinted. 'I don't understand.'

'They're just words.'

'No, I mean, I don't understand the numbers. This is not the work Jules was doing.'

'Are you sure?'

'He showed me his early workings,' Lars said. 'First drafts, notes. This isn't it. This is the lottery, perhaps. It's only numbers.'

He lowered the page for me to see. It was true: it was just numbers. They didn't look any smarter than when I first saw them. *Anyway freedom goodbye.* I felt like I was going to vomit.

'I'm sorry,' I said. 'I made a mistake.'

'I've already told the investors the product will not be delivered.' He shook his head. 'To be honest, I expected this failure. I have watched for a long time while his talent was eroded. It's no good.'

'You'd better go,' I said.

'If you've done nothing wrong, Sam, you should come forward. The longer you wait, the worse it will be for you.'

'I've done just enough for that to be impossible.' I looked at the numbers. 'Jules and I used to talk about dark matter, but you know what? This is the dark matter.'

Lars looked at me. He stood up and took off his jacket.

'You're a conspicuous mess,' he said. 'Put this on.'

'I'm not coming.'

'I know. So you must not get cold. It will be a few days before I can get the papers ready.'

His jacket was thin and light, like silk. It slid easily over my damp, bloody shirt.

'What if it stains?'

'This suit is very old,' he said. 'I keep it because the cloth is a good weight for all weathers. See here? Somebody spilled wine on it. And here? I fell, stoned. Rolled across a road in Hong Kong. The sleeve and side panel all torn up – it was no good. I said, it is ruined, but the tailor said, no way. He insisted. And can you see where it has been repaired? No. It's good work. But it's damaged. It will never be good, really.'

I put my things in the pockets. I rolled up my jacket and hid it in a corner.

'I really appreciate this, Lars. How long will it take to get the passport?'

'Two, maybe three days. Unfortunately I cannot offer you a place to stay, however.'

'Could you give me a lift?'

He hesitated.

'I'll lie down in the back seat.'

'Of course, Sam. Of course.'

I waited inside the cemetery fence while he got the car. When he drove up I popped the back door and climbed inside. It was hard not to fall asleep as I stretched out. Benny Goodman was bouncing on the radio.

'I was listening to the news but you are up to date with the headlines,' he said. 'Where shall we go?'

I got him to drive up K Road. The billboards were unlit but I could see Lucy's giant hand above me as it slid past. There were police cars patrolling the busiest corners. Lars had to slow down. There was a lot of foot traffic.

'Sex is a release in times of tension,' he said.

'Tell me when it's safe to look.'

'There are people everywhere.'

'Circle the block.'

I peeked out the window. Sirens were flashing behind one of the strip clubs. Lucy was standing just down from the corner wearing a leotard under her orange fur. Lars pulled up and called her over to the window. He had to show a lot of bills before she'd get in. I got him to drop us a block away from her apartment.

'You two kids have fun,' he said.

Chapter 20

The power was still off in Lucy's building. Our footsteps echoed up the fire escape. She wasn't certain that having me stay at her place was a good idea but I flashed the bottles in my pocket and she said yes. I was carrying what she needed to be happy. I didn't mention the money or the cards she had stolen from me but she didn't seem nervous about it. She talked as if we were meeting for the first time. When I mentioned her billboard she didn't respond, either. She dropped her coat on the apartment floor and told me she wanted something straight away.

I set it out for her in the bathroom. While she was doing it, I checked the locks. I jammed a rolled-up magazine under the door. Lucy sat in the bedroom unstrapping her platforms and making jokes about people I didn't know. The snake tattoo was still curled around her arm.

She thought I was there to fuck her but I wasn't. I couldn't. I didn't want to and I had forgotten how. There was nothing arousing about her dry, boyish body. She rubbed against me with animal impatience but got nothing from it either as far as I could tell. She had no smell or taste. The things she said and did were just part of her routine. Her secret life was like the apartment with nothing in it: it would have been shocking if everyone else didn't live like that. Her days were ordinary except they passed in the space of an hour. She was younger than I'd first thought, if she had ever been young.

She moved constantly in the bed, keeping me awake. She pressed my back, bit the backs of my arms, my wrists, the flesh of my palms. She slipped her thumbnail along my spine, fingernails dancing. The tickling sensation spread up my back, along the indentations in my skin. She traced the scars along the peak of my shoulder. She folded into me, recumbent and warm. I shivered, only half awake. I had a dream about a geisha speaking in a language I didn't understand, her red gown slipping in the steam, her hair lank and tangled around my fingers.

Dawn was coming up. The light was the colour of cornflour. The traffic sounded like gentle rain. Somewhere between sleeping and waking she had slipped out of the bed and left me alone. Beyond the Chrysler Building the Eiffel Tower was fading in the sun. I was dreaming a lullaby: a girl singing 'Sweet Jane', her faint voice stretching to reach the notes. Na na na na na, sweet Jane. And then it really was a voice.

I got up and went to the door. Lucy was standing in the lounge dancing nude in front of the window, her hands hugging her skinny brown shoulders in the sunrise. She was stepping to the song's beat as she kissed her hands, the tips of her fingers, the touch of her lips describing something imagined by her own warm body and its interwoven chemical rushes.

Na na na na na, sweet Jane.

She looked at me like I was just another dozy thought.

'Hello baby,' she said.

'No one else knows we're here – yeah?'

'Sure.'

The way she said it wasn't right but I expected that. It didn't prove she was lying.

'And nobody's watching us?' I said.

'They could be working on it,' she said. 'The CIA have groups of psychics to look into people's minds.'

'Looking into my mind wouldn't tell anyone anything. It's like a map folded up wrong. The city doesn't make sense. I can recognise some places but I'm still lost.'

She smiled at me. 'You're in such a great place, honey.'

I pointed out the window. 'Jules grew up in Paris. Do you see? And Candy and Jules met in New York.'

'That's so cool,' she said. 'Maybe you shouldn't straighten out. Maybe if you stay loose they won't be able to get into your mind. And you'll be safe.'

'I need a bill.'

She shook out her fake fur. Coins bounced on the carpet.

'I loved it when they changed from notes to coins,' she said. 'With notes you spend them and they're gone but with coins you wake up in the morning and there's a whole other night in your pocket.'

I chopped a pill into the line. She gave me a fifty-dollar bill and I rolled it up.

'We need to talk,' I said.

Lucy was getting a little colder now. She put her coat back on and sat cross-legged on the floor holding her fingertips under her nose, the other hand cupped around her cunt as if everything rushing inside her might spill out.

'How did you end up here, Lucy?' I said.

'Your friend in the car.'

'In Auckland, I mean. Did you choose to come here?'

'Of course I did. Didn't you?'

I laughed.

'You think that's funny?'

'Sure. I mean, you're right. Here I am, the same situation as you . . .'

'I came here for work,' she sniffed. 'Different sort of work, but, you know.'

'Yes.'

'And this was better. Better work, I think. I've saved a lot of money.'

'That's good. So you can go any time.'

'Sure I can.'

'You mean it?'

She made a face. 'I need a passport.'

'They took your passport?'

'Yeah. I mean, I can get it but I'd have to pay money.'

I leaned over and pulled her collar down. She looked puzzled.

'Your tattoo,' I said. 'Helen Anyway had one like it. You know Helen?'

'Yeah, so?'

'Did you know she's dead?'

'She OD'd.'

'I was with her in the hotel.'

Lucy's eyes were already too wide. She twitched and cleared her throat. I kept talking in a low voice. I didn't want her to panic.

'I just want you to be safe,' I said. 'I saw what happened to her, and I don't want that to happen to you.'

She glared at me across her knuckles.

'I'm sure you know who I'm talking about,' I said. 'I know you've promised to keep quiet. But I'm thinking that if I could just go see this person, maybe talk to them, then I can be sure there's no misunderstanding.'

'You mustn't tell.'

'I won't.'

'You can't tell.'

'I can get you a new passport.'

I kept giving her reasons and they kept getting shakier and then finally she folded. But she still didn't want to say it out loud so she took out a lipstick and wrote the number on the skin around my wrist.

★ ★ ★

She was tired enough to sleep. I drew the curtains and dimmed the room and put her back in bed with her coat laid over the top of her as a blanket. She was murmuring and warm and feeling good about herself now.

I shut myself in the bathroom and sat down on the floor. I used Helen Anyway's phone. He picked up after it rang fourteen times.

'Goodbye,' he said.

'It's not Helen,' I said.

'I know that.' There was a noise – not breathing, but something else. The noise of his mouth: he was chewing gum.

'So we should get together,' he said. 'Sort things out.'

The pauses made it sound like he was distracted but when he spoke I could tell I was the only thing on his mind.

We sat on the phone listening to one another saying nothing. I didn't know what to do. Was there a protocol to observe?

'There's a place called the Sky Room,' he said. 'Tonight.' And then he hung up.

He knew Helen Anyway was dead, and he knew I had her phone, and he knew Lucy. That was enough information to have me tracked down and arrested. But instead he'd waited for me to contact him first. He was reaching out to me. He hadn't gone to the cops because he and I were on the same side.

Mr Goodbye.

I stood up and opened the door and went out and

climbed into bed. Lucy was still saying something to herself. My skin tingled when she touched it. I wanted to succumb to the apartment and its stupid, drowsy pleasures: the rhythm of sleep and drugs and elevation, stasis and balance – but it wasn't time for that yet.

Chapter 21

I got up at night and had a shower and cleaned the worst of the mud off my clothes. I used the kitchen bench to strip the gun and wipe off the sea salt that had collected on the mechanism. It would rust soon and be too dangerous to fire. I didn't know where I would be then.

Lucy came out into the lounge. She had put on pin-lined jeans and a silver top that exposed her belly and her hair was in pigtails. She started changing the candles, lighting them with a transparent Zippo that had tiny diodes flashing inside it. I asked if she knew the Sky Room.

'It's uptown. They've got power there.'

'I'm going to meet Goodbye. I need you to walk me there just as far as the door. I'll look after you.'

'Like you looked after Helen?'

'Just as far as the door and that's it.'

I snapped back the slide. I pulled the trigger and the empty chamber clicked. There were three remaining rounds. I slid them into the magazine. Lucy smiled as if it was a game.

'That's a sweet little gun,' she said. 'My friend's got one like that.'

I waited but she kept smiling. Either she couldn't work it out or she didn't want to.

I made her take me out through the back of the building. The brick walls of the alley had been smoothed by acid rain. The streets were crowded with people and sharp sounds. I got distracted trying to cross the road and was nearly run down. I was looking in the windows and at the signs, trying to count the white and pink spots of chewing gum pressed into the bitumen. When we got close I pulled Lucy aside and we had another bump, just to be safe.

The Sky Room was a four-storey building rising above a fenced triangle of park ground. People were scattered across it like litter, lounging around the trees and benches as if the sun was still shining. They didn't blink as we walked between them. They all had the same glazed stare.

There wasn't a queue at the door, or a sign. The music coming from inside was loud. Lucy pressed her face against the ticket glass and shouted something and the girl nodded and let us in.

A spiral staircase twisted up inside the building. I put my arm around Lucy and held her tight and we went up.

The bass was shaking the steps. On the first floor were red-lit doors and people dancing to the same song in different rooms. Lucy stared at the moving bodies. I shouted at her that this was a good place to split up: she would be safer in a crowd. I let go of her waist and put the stuff in her hands and started to thank her but she was already stepping into the crowd. She didn't look back and I didn't blame her for it.

Some people came down the other way, giggling as they fumbled past in the dark. The next landing was blue, lit by UV. Pale things bobbed to the rhythm. I had to feel my way from there. The handrail kept going.

The top floor was wide with a low ceiling. There were couches down one side and booths on the other and lamps on the tables and velvet paintings of eagles and tigers. Elvis was singing 'Wooden Heart' on the old Wurlitzer jukebox. There was a line of pool tables down the middle of the room but nobody was playing. People were lying on seats, smoking, talking.

I chose a booth that let me see people as they came in through the door. In the next booth along was a girl in a silver top, the sort of thing Lucy would wear. She was sitting with two boys who also looked familiar, but I didn't know from where. One of them lit her cigarette for her. They weren't talking. The three of them were just sitting there, letting the room flow over them.

I put my feet up. I brushed the tassels on the lampshade. Everything was coming on again, big waves and then bigger. The jukebox was playing 'Cinnamon Girl'. Gradually people fell back into the shadows. The two boys and their silver girl left.

I could tell it was Goodbye when he walked in.

He was broad and stocky, wearing cowboy boots and black jeans, and his fists sparkled with a ring on every finger – silver, turquoise, cut stones. His skin was tanned and stretched like new leather. He had a square jaw and a cleft in his chin. He was wearing aviator sunglasses and chewing gum, and his white stare escaped each time he sucked back his spittle. His long hair was in a ponytail and his hairline was very black and very perfect.

I blinked.

'You a light sleeper?' he said.

I nodded. My mouth was filled with cotton balls. I couldn't answer.

'I can tell just by looking: light sleeper. I hear things, too. I got eyes and ears all over. Top fucking dollar. That's my job. To know what goes on. I keep tabs on everything. Always looking. You doze off and that's it – game over. You've got no control when you sleep. That's how I know.'

He rapped the table to call the meeting to attention but the music kept playing and people kept squirming in their booths.

'So,' he said. 'Nice to meet you.'

'I like meeting people.'

He waved at the room. 'I guess you know everyone.'

'I do. But they're so young, I don't know what to say to them. They bore me.'

'Maybe you bore them.'

'You seem interesting, though.'

'Cheers.'

'I bet you meet lots of people.'

'All the time. I pick my friends.'

'Why's that?'

'I have to be careful.'

'Oh come on,' I said. 'Don't give me that. What else are you going to do?'

'Maybe go home. Read a book.'

'I read the letter,' I said, sitting up a little taller in the booth. I scratched my cheek: his stare was like a black fly crawling up it.

'I just wanted to let you know,' I said.

'Where is it?'

'It's safe. No one's going to find it.'

'Who's read it?'

'A couple of people. But they don't know what it means.'

'But you do.'

'I just thought you'd want it back.'

The jukebox clicked and switched songs again. The booth glowed with a lazy light.

Goodbye rapped the table top again.

'Let's cruise back to my place,' he said.

The stairs spiralled all the way down to the basement where an old black Peugeot was parked by the door. Two kids were sitting on the hood. They threw down their cigarettes and stood up when they saw us coming. One had bleached hair and one was shaven bald. I recognised them without their ties: the guys who I'd found waiting outside my apartment.

'Who the fuck are you?' Goodbye said.

'I'm Matt,' said the bleached kid. 'You know.'

Goodbye pointed at the other one.

'Then who's this?'

'He's Mark.'

'Mark?' Goodbye wiped the back of his neck. 'Was there a Mark?'

'You remember, sir,' Mark said.

'Don't be a fucking smart ass,' Goodbye said. 'I'm the one who says what I fucking recall.'

Matt lifted the roller door. Goodbye peered up at the sky and the stars. The moon looked like grey sand.

'What is it?' I said.

'The army's got fucking satellites everywhere, flying around. They can see right in your fucking window. Day and night, twenty-four hours. They're like the all-seeing eye of God. They know where everything is.'

Goodbye and I sat in the back. Matt got in the front and Mark started the car and pulled out sharply into the lane behind the building. He stomped on the accelerator without turning on the headlights and drove fast down the lane and out on to the road. Goodbye leaned forward.

'Where the fuck are we now?' he said.

'It's not far.'

'Are you sure?'

I couldn't tell where we were going. Mark was taking directions from Matt, hanging off the column shift and punching up through the gears, one hand on the wheel. Matt whispered something and pointed and Mark threw the old car sharp around another corner.

We came up to a rise and drove through the open gates of a high stone wall and into a brilliant red light from the burning torches. A long driveway curved up towards a low, split-level mansion, its windows reflecting the flames.

'Where's this?' Goodbye said. 'Is this the place?'

'This is it,' Matt said.

'This is it? What sort of place is it? Who built this? Did I build it?'

'It was built by a guy who made lemonade in the seventies.'

'Jesus Christ.' He spat his gum out the window. 'Is it safe?'

'It's got an alarm.'

'What's the fucking code? Do I know it? Jesus.'

'We know it.'

Mark stopped the car at the end of the driveway and killed the engine. Goodbye shut his eyes and let his big head roll on his shoulders. Nobody moved. We all just sat there, the boys staring ahead. Light danced across us all, licking the car with long orange flames. Goodbye took a fistful of wrappers and notes out of his pocket and started picking through them.

'So you're sure this is where I live?' he said.

'Yep,' Matt said.

'Do I like it here?'

'It's okay. But you're looking at other places.'

Goodbye found a fresh piece of gum and unwrapped it and put it in his mouth.

'So what's the code?' he said.

'The alarm and the gates don't work. There's a generator inside.'

'Huh.' He looked at the white house, chewing, then jerked his thumb at me.

'So who is this guy?' he asked.

'That's Samuel Usher.'

'Why's he here?'

'He's a mate of Jules.'

'He's the one who got the letter,' Goodbye said.

Matt shrugged. 'Yeah?'

Goodbye hit him. He reached forward fast and slapped the boy so hard he was thrown back in the seat and smashed against the dashboard. Nobody moved. Matt hunched. Goodbye opened the door with his red hand.

'Shake a leg,' he said.

He stepped out and walked unsteady to the door, hands stuffed in his jacket pockets.

My legs were shaking and my eyes were starting to close again. Mark helped me across the gravel. His hands smelled of kerosene and mint-flavoured spit.

Chapter 22

Inside it looked like the crowd from the Sky Room had got there ahead of us. The house was built around an open courtyard with a pool and every space was filled with people. The glass doors were shaking with huge, looping techno. Candles threw up crazy shadows across desert plants and patterned walls and the air was thick with incense and sweat. Kids were dancing and shimmying on the floor, stripped down in the heat. They had dumped powders and pills on a big smoked-glass table and were slithering in piles around it, the candle light greasing their necks.

Goodbye led me past the hallway aquarium filled with tropical goldfish and tangled weeds. He opened a mirrored drinks cabinet and scooped up the white rails in his fingertips, wadding his nostrils. I took the bill and did a line and stopped halfway to gag. It was like sticking an ice-pick up my nose. My eyes were streaming and my upper lip was spotted with blood. I choked and cleared my throat and finished and then the noises and smells and lights came alive and everything was hard and cool and perfect.

'You like to shoot?' Goodbye said.

'Sometimes.'

'Come see this,' he said.

He took me downstairs. The basement room was walled with scoria. There were more candles burning beneath the full-body targets at the end of the shooting gallery. At the back of the room was a wide rack of guns: forty, fifty pieces laid out in pine boxes and cloth-and-steel trays. I hesitated.

'Go ahead,' he said.

I picked up the nearest one. It was short, and fat, and colder to handle than it looked.

'Spanish Astra,' he said. 'That's a fighting dog.'

I picked up a Glock.

'Looks like a kid's toy, doesn't it?' Goodbye said. 'Like it's no threat at all.'

He watched me fish out another automatic.

'Israeli Desert Eagle. That's a military piece, no bullshit. But if you want something with real pedigree, check out this.'

He opened a varnished wooden case. Inside it, against the red velvet, were matched duelling pistols trimmed in fluttering brass and silver.

'Boutet,' he said. 'Napoleonic period. Have a go.'

I carefully picked one out, held it with two hands.

'Quite a weight, huh?' He grinned. 'It's designed to be muzzle-heavy. The weight controls the recoil, helps you aim. You need that if your hands are shaking – especially if it's your first time.' He ran a stubby finger around the mechanism. 'The hammer comes down on the frizzen, here – sparks the ignition charge, that sparks the propellant. The frizzen's a roller, not a plate, so the spark will always

179

catch. More reliable: you won't misfire. And it's a hair trigger: precise. Because this is a precise art. The art of the duel.'

He picked up the second pistol and aimed it between my eyes.

'You master your nerves,' he said. 'You have to be precise. Your weapon must discharge at the referee's call: not before, not too late. You stand straight, sideways, offering the minimum target. The smoke from the ignition will hide you before you fire: if your opponent's nervous, he won't wait for it to clear – he'll fire as soon as he sees the smoke and he'll miss. If you're disciplined, dedicated – you win. Stay calm, clear your mind, hone your reactions, wait for the moment . . . and release. A bullet is intention. It moves in a straight line. No fuck-ups.'

'Bullets tumble,' I said.

'These? Sure. They fire a lead ball.'

'No – any bullet can tumble. The trajectory is decaying from the moment of release. Anything can throw off a bullet. A piece of curtain fabric. A sheet of paper. I mean, it's probably going to hit, but it's not a certainty. Everything is subject to turbulence.'

Goodbye smiled.

'I've heard all about it,' he said. 'I knew a guy who talked about that all the time – how things always decay, always fuck up, how everything will inevitably spin out of control, but you know what? That's a load of bullshit. The real world works the same way it always did.'

★ ★ ★

We went upstairs and he pushed open the glass door and led me into the courtyard. The pool was filled with white water that wasn't reflecting the moon. There were puddles between the paving stones where people had been splashing around. Goodbye stepped straight off the edge, but instead of sinking he descended in stages like he was sliding down steps. I touched the whiteness. It was dry. Instead of water, the pool was filled with plastic packing foam.

The white pieces stuck to me as I followed him in. I was getting hot. I pulled off my jacket and shirt and slumped against the side to breathe. Goodbye looked at my shoulder.

'What'd you take for it?' he said. 'Did they do a graft?'

'No graft.'

'That's why it's all puckered up,' he said. 'Flesh doesn't stretch by itself.'

He stared at me through the thick mask of his skin.

'At one time, everybody knew me,' he said. 'Not any more.'

My heart was thumping.

'See, it's not you who's in trouble,' he said. 'It's your face. What people see. So you get rid of it, pay someone to put you under the knife. They tell you which hotel. You check in, you wait. Then you get a call and go downstairs – immediately. If you're in the shower you walk out just in a towel.

'First time I only made small changes – nose, around the eyes. Then I got into a new line of business, new clients – pretty soon I had to leave them, too. That happened a couple of times. I think I'm settled now, for the moment. But who knows? I miss it. That last hour is the best fucking feeling in the world. So much tension has been building up you could go like that. Like *that*. But the hour before, you turn to ice. You know soon you'll wake up and you'll be gone. Every time before I go under the knife I take one last look in the mirror and say, Goodbye mister. That's you finished with. That's the end of it.'

I snapped my fingers: 'Just like that.'

'Just like that.' He grinned. 'Every time I change my diet, what I drink, my whole intake: electrolytes, carbohydrates, the whole fucking thing. I change my body's balance, my aura. And I change drugs because I don't want the same fucking feelings back about the colour blue or some bitch or whatever. Like I know I need the coke again now, I don't mind that and I don't give a fuck that it's making me talk, because I need to talk. But the last two times I moved right away from that, and again maybe once before.' He smiled. 'Oh yeah, four or five times. Actually I think I lost fucking count.

'First time, I hated myself so bad, so bad.' He shook his head. 'Total antidepressant fuck-up. Librium and thorazine cut with diazepam. Munched them for fucking breakfast. Second time I had nausea again so I had to slow down and warm up: Benadryl, Colanadine, painkillers. A lot of hash.

My hands swelled up like a boxer. That's who I was: a tired fighter, Sam. I was so fucked up.'

There was a row of little phials on the rim of the pool. He picked one and stuffed it under his nose and snorted deep, closing his eyes.

'I hate when I remember,' he said softly. 'The past is over. It has nothing to do with me now. Now all that interests me is the moment, and young skin.'

He passed me the phial. The sweat on my chest felt like tears. And then the stupor hit me double-, triple-time. Relaxation flowed across me gentle and rich, the noise of dancing and fucking and laughter, and love, and happiness, drum fills and breathing. I was sitting there trying to work out if I was feeling good and then, abruptly, I did.

It's that easy. That's all it is. We're just vessels. We carry all these chemicals in our body and some of them make us happy and some of them make us sad. The same goes for intelligence and spatial depth and pretty colours and time. It's a scientific fact: we're just chemicals running through a brain. The only memories we have are enzymes and sugar: when they break up your past breaks up and goes with it – your past, your present, everything.

Goodbye blinked, heavy-lidded, talking to me through the wingspan of his hands.

'This is a business,' he said. 'I'm a businessman. And business is good. You have Prohibition in the twenties, so things go underground and the syndicates get strong. Then World War II, governments are scared of communism – they'll do a deal with anybody. The CIA builds landing strips all around here, builds the export partnerships – there's a whole new distribution network in place. And now business goes global. Suddenly all these countries open up, everyone's talking to each other. People in London are doing what people in Los Angeles are doing. One world, one market. It's beautiful. I've never seen anything like it. Unprecedented. We're posting fifteen thousand per cent. How about that – fifteen *thousand*. Who else gives that kind of return? Nobody.'

I had stopped listening. He thought he knew who he was talking to, but he didn't. He was just talking to someone who looked like me. Who looked like Jules, who looked like Candy, who looked like everybody else. Very slowly, I started to get up.

'You're leaving?' he said.

'Just like that.'

He grinned like that was funnier than it was.

I let it ride.

I climbed out of the pool and buttoned my shirt and stood up and left him spread out in the half-light. I walked across the courtyard.

The music in the lounge was getting louder. Pills had been trodden into the carpet. The kids were stamping the floor, knocking over the candles. I reached for the front door but it magically opened. Matt was standing on the other side, smiling, and Mark was standing by a car parked in the driveway. Lucy was in the front seat. She was hauling herself up on the steering wheel. Blood was pouring across her face, cherry red in the flames. Her movements were automatic and horrible. She felt her way across the front seat like a half-crushed insect, smearing crimson on the glass.

Mark threw me the keys. I missed catching them: they hit me in the chest and bounced to the ground. I had to get on my hands and knees to pick them up. Standing, I was so dizzy I nearly fell down again. Matt slapped me on the shoulder.

'We figured you'd be okay to drive,' he said.

Chapter 23

I pulled over in a quiet street at the bottom of the hill. There were no bird songs, no traffic. Everything was asleep except for us. The city had become a maze, fog obscuring the landmarks. Lucy's purse was on the floor and her things had been thrown around the back seat. I picked up her phone.

'Who are you calling?' she said.

'Nobody.' I cupped my hand over the receiver.

There was a roar in the sky and a plane shot out above the trees. A big, silver twin-propeller DC-3, the passenger windows painted over. It made a low, gleaming sweep over the park and flew away over the city, the sound of its engines fading. Lucy giggled and reached up to touch it.

'Flew away,' she said. As she spoke the wounds in her face broke open fresh.

I finished the call and started picking up her things to put back in her purse but the bag had been ripped almost in half. I dropped it all and walked around outside the car and opened her door.

'Where's the Carnival from here?' I said.

She pointed, squinting through the eye that wasn't closed.

★ ★ ★

We made our way across the park and then into the streets. Walking felt like the ground was going to give way any second. I pulled her close to stop us both shivering as we walked. She was warm, her own muscles going into spasm. Her perfume smelled fresh, her sweat clean.

She looked more naked as the light got brighter. One side of her hair had fallen out of the plait and her thigh flashed out of the torn pants leg with each step. Teenage boys stared as she passed: she would have looked good to their warm, pink minds. As we got closer she noticed the tear and tried to hold the two halves together.

'You okay?'

'I'm fine,' she said.

There was a queue outside the Carnival. Generator wires were running downstairs to the lights and sound system. Lucy combed her hair across her face with her fingernails. I waved cash so we could jump the line. The woman on the coat check let us in.

Lars was waiting by the door, watching the westerns playing on the set behind the counter. He stubbed his cigarette out on the wet top when he saw us come in. I walked Lucy straight past him to a corner where she could slide in and keep the bad side of her face to the wall.

Lars brought drinks over to the table. He glanced at the sweat and mud I had collected and then at Lucy with her hand over her face.

'It's been a while,' he said. 'But you haven't changed.'

'I fucked up your jacket.'

He shook his head. 'I said it's no worry. I am surprised there isn't a dress code, you know?' He winked. 'They are saying power will be restored to most of the city soon. It's a little bit of a shame, don't you think? It's been exciting for people. A little break from their routine.'

It didn't feel like a break. It felt like people doing what they always did, faster and faster. A glassie collecting bottles in a bucket knocked the edge of the table. Lars caught our drinks before they spilled. A blonde girl was dancing in the crowd, swaying in other men's arms.

'Did you help Candy when she left?' I said.

'Yes. Not that she needed help. Anyone can leave – it's a free country. I helped her find a job.'

'And what did she say?'

'Nothing about you. But in my experience this is a good sign. People never discuss what matters to them. They love music and nights like this but they would never say. They talk as if good things never happen to them. They forget the good things.'

'Is she okay?'

He smiled to break the news that was obvious to everybody except me. 'Look at yourself, Sam,' he said.

'I know.'

'Let's go, yes?'

I touched Lucy's shoulder. She gave a start and then slumped back against the wall. There were worse places to go into shock than a warm club in the early hours but there were better places, too. I shouted to Lars.

'This is Lucy. I need you to get her to a doctor. She works and she's about seventeen.'

'Sure thing,' he said.

I spoke into her ear.

'Goodbye,' I said. 'Where does he meet people?'

'The car wash. He picks people up and drives through. The one down on Stanley Street – Freedom Car Wash.'

I stared at Lucy. She repeated herself, thinking I hadn't heard. *Anyway freedom goodbye.* The things he breathed and loved. I was lying when I told Goodbye I understood it, but now I did understand.

I told Lars to go.

'You're not coming?' he said.

'I'll catch up.'

He frowned. I helped Lucy sit up.

'I'm not a prostitute,' she said.

'Lars and I were talking about something else.'

'I'm twenty-one.'

Lars helped her up and they left, climbing the steps that rose all the way into the night.

I went into the toilets and shut myself in a cubicle and sat down. My mind was moving faster now: I was waking up. *Anyway freedom goodbye*: the contact, the place and the source.

Goodbye was Jules' dealer from way back, and Jules had a bad debt. Jules couldn't raise the money to repay it, naturally. He was blowing his shitty job at the university. He had promised Lars he could crack a high-tech job that nobody else could – an algorithm that brought the earth closer. It was a fantasy. Jules was fried and raving: he couldn't think. He and Candy both knew where it was going. They were stupid but they weren't fools. She even met with Goodbye to see what could be done. She was sitting with him in the Normandy the day I met her – he was the big guy with the ponytail, the face nobody looked at. He was probably on to me right from that day.

Jules decided to buy time. He needed leverage. He needed times and places, a record of transactions.

Goodbye met people in a car wash. They got in the car and drove through and the noise of the machinery hid them from surveillance. All Jules did was record the codes for the car-wash tickets, his and everybody else's.

That was it. It was all just numbers. The army had no satellites and the CIA couldn't see into people's minds. The end of the world is just numbers.

Candy had already packed. Candy was already leaving: she and I were the last thing she did. I had been holding back and waiting and circling and she was already gone, kissing me while the sun was falling.

Jules would have met with Goodbye. He would have shown him the numbers and talked a lot, laying things out as he thought they were. By advancing theories we construct the world anew: I describe it, and so it becomes that way. Except not this time, because Goodbye tapped him in the car wash and left him wet on the side of the road. And here, Jules had two options: give up the numbers or not.

Jules' back-up plan was to send me the numbers and Goodbye's back-up plan was to send a hot dose courtesy of Helen Anyway. They had challenged each other across time and place to a duel at two different dawns. Except Jules' body was weak. He never woke up.

There must have been a time when my hands didn't shake but I couldn't remember it. It might as well have been my first time. You master your nerves because this is a precise art. If you are disciplined you will win.

Jules loved a trajectory. The magic bullet, the silver bullet – that's all people talk about, have you noticed? Why do we love bullets and shells?

Because a bullet is intention.

I took the baby nine out of my pocket and turned it over, looking at it, touching each part with a fingertip, memorising it, recording the shapes. I clutched it. I could almost hide it in my hand. I tore the left pocket of Lars' jacket a little so I could draw it without snagging the sight on the fabric. I slipped out the magazine and counted the bullets again where they lay in their narrow metal slot, all lined up.

I stood up and went out and splashed cold water on my face. I was pale in the mirror. I had always been pale.

★ ★ ★

In the Carnival the music was charging up bodies, making the dancers awake and vibrant, their skin tender and warm. Everything was whirling in a drug frenzy, speed jitters and lockjaw propped awake by the music and women's backs glowing soft and fabulous. For the whole night they'd been running off the constant buzz of lines and pills and shots and powders and now the music was good and their lives were brilliantly lit and time would never come to an end.

Because time never will end, now. As long as there is light and heat there is no difference between night and day. Electricity permits us to lead these unnatural lives: to live nights like they are days, winter like summer, to deny that the planet is turning and we are all adrift in the ether.

Chapter 24

I started walking towards Stanley Street. A police car came down K Road and I ducked behind a bus stop until it had passed and left the street sounding longer and emptier than before. I started walking again. The gun's tiny weight was swinging in my pocket. I was thinking about how many times I had walked around here at lunchtime, but the streets were different now it was night. Time made this a whole different place.

I could see the neon Freedom sign a long way off. The car wash was attached to a gas station at the bottom of the hill. The forecourt was covered by a metal awning as wide as a field, the fluorescent lights gently shaking the cement. There was only one attendant on duty, a fat guy reading a newspaper inside a security booth made of shatter-proof glass. The holes drilled through the panes sat level with the rubber band around his wrist and the blackened nail on his thumb. The public phone was hanging outside on the wall in a clear perspex bubble. I used it to call the number and leave a message and sat down on the verge to wait. The lights painted the grass the colour of milk.

In my head the phone rang twice a minute. Each

time I stood up and took the receiver off the hook and listened for the dial tone. I must have stood up to check and sat down again a dozen times. Finally it rang for real. The kid on the other end told me to buy a ticket and wait. I hung up.

I went to the security booth and spoke through the holes to buy a car wash. The attendant used a two-way metal drawer to take my money and slide the ticket out. He must have watched me come into the station on foot but he didn't say anything about it. A line of video monitors sat behind him above the counter. The back of my head was on camera. I walked away looking down to hide my face.

The car wash was a metal frame the size of a double garage. The sides were walled with frosted glass and the roof was hung with oily-looking flaps and pneumatic hoses. I stood by the entrance counting the windows in the warehouse across the road. I checked the gun, wiped my palms. I didn't think about walking away. Squinting, I could still see the Chrysler Building. I knew it wasn't there, but I could see it.

The big black Peugeot was running with its headlamps switched off. As it glided out of the darkness my reflection snaked across the windows. It pulled into the wash lane and stopped close enough for me to bring out the gun and squeeze three bullets through the tinted glass but I didn't. I opened the passenger door and got in.

Goodbye was behind the wheel, and he was alone. He watched as I glanced at the back seat to check. He didn't blink. He tapped the wheel with his pinky ring.

'Wash or wax?' he said.

'Deluxe wax.'

He drove up to the control box that guarded the wash and wound his window down.

'What's the number?'

I read out the five numbers on the ticket and he punched the keys. The box blinked and the illuminated sign at the entrance told us to drive in. He wound up the window and tapped the accelerator and drove into the jaws of the machine. The sign said stop and clamps locked the front wheels into place and an articulated arm swung towards us across the bonnet of the car. As it moved up the windscreen the light before us softened and turned to silver ribbons that twisted down the glass.

Goodbye turned and looked across the shadows at me.

'It's not easy to do,' he said. 'It's easy to have the idea and talk about it. Everyone has their own theory about what they'd do in this situation, how far they'd go. But when it really comes down to it, it's a lot harder than you think.'

My hand was still in my pocket. I had got into the car to do the right thing but that was the reason everyone would give. We are all trying to do the right thing. You can move a long way off beam before you realise what has happened. Most of the people you see and talk to every day are on the verge of doing something very bad indeed. All it takes is that little bit extra that pushes them over the edge. A word; the flick of a switch. And afterwards people scratch their heads and ask: how did someone become that way – how did they go down that irrational path? But the fact is there are a million paths and a million places we slip up.

We are tasked at an atomic level.

The spraying arm had moved behind us. It stopped and folded away like a mantis and then two smaller sisters unfolded and began spraying the wheels and rocker panels. The drumming noise swept around us.

'Listen,' Goodbye said. 'Come back to my place. I have chandoo aged like whisky, in porcelain jars stopped with cork and beeswax – beautiful things, you'd love these jars. Thirty, forty years old. We'll crack one open. We'll talk it out.'

The rocker set stopped and clacked and started moving back around the car.

'Like I said, it's a business,' Goodbye said. 'People say it's a problem: something that should be stopped, something that can be treated, but it's so much bigger than that. It's an entire culture, an economy, a whole language. People who see the world without it aren't really seeing the world at all. They aren't even looking. Because if they could see the world, what it's really like, they would see that this thing is not just a part of it – it's the whole fucking basis of it. We're the land and the sea. Everyone's in on it. And who wouldn't want to be? It's a business. People get hurt?' He shrugged. 'People get hurt crossing the road.'

The drumming faded and big white drops of soap fell on the glass. The soft bursts ran down my hand.

There were so many reasons to do nothing. If I fired, the ejected cartridge would be marked by the firing pin and the bullet would be scored by the barrel. My fingerprints were on the cartridge and the gun. There would be powder burns and residue on my sleeve. The attendant had seen me buy the ticket. The back of my head was on the video screen. I used the phone: touched the handset and the keys. It's so easy to track somebody down. All you need is half a name or a blurred picture and then everything starts to fall into place. I knew because I'd done it myself dozens of times. And if I turned up dead, the unidentified body would be held at the central morgue with all the other people found on the street. The state pays for a slot in the freezer, the certification, the tests, the trace. Everyone is taken care of.

'The secret,' he said, 'is stability. Just keep everything ticking over. Play the averages. Keep things running smooth. That's what I do. I make sure things run smoothly: everything's in order and nothing fucks up. Sweet as.'

Stability. Calm. A continuum. Everything that is not in nature.

I took out the gun and pointed it at his head, an inch away from his temple. He kept looking past it, at me. He was breathing slowly. His big hands stayed resting on the wheel.

'One of my cooks,' he said, 'did a runner. The money I spent on that fucker you wouldn't believe. We moved the lab every week – you know what that cost? It's not like you get rent-a-truck, you know? You have to pay guys to keep their fucking mouths shut. You know how I did it? I got a friend in rental property. Every week he'd evict a different student flat and we'd move the lab in. Cost a fortune. But it was worth it, keeping ahead. We were in profit.

'Then this prick ups and runs with a month's goods. One month. Pisses off to Sydney. After everything I've done. Fucked if I know why – thinks he's gonna start over, or some bullshit. So then I had to go find him. I would've liked someone else to do it, but it had to be me. Do you know what it takes to drill a guy's kneecaps? You've gotta tie him down. You can gag him all you want but you still hear the screams – nothing's gonna muffle that. You have to find a basement, or a moving truck. You have to get an electric drill, and a bit, and you plug in the drill and then press the trigger . . .' He pointed his finger at me. 'And then you have to push and feel and watch the fucking thing going through the skin and bone and gristle. The bit bites and the whole thing twists in your fucking hands. You can smell it burning. And he's pissing and screaming and kicking. You do it, and you think you're gonna die. And then you finish and pull it out and it's like time has stood still. And you know what happens then? You realise you're only half done.'

I pulled the trigger and the gun went off as loud as a bomb and his head snapped back and a blood-purple rose splattered on the window and the noise in my ear was like a hammer on wood.

Goodbye's blood and brains were running down the inside of the glass, shadowing the soap as it was washed away, the hot wax buffered by whirring fans, the car rocking in its pneumatic cradle as it was dried and shined. His body lost its grip on the seat and slid forward and I could smell shit and piss and blood.

I took the phone out of my pocket and dropped it. I opened the car door and stepped out into the falling water.

The warm soap was still running from the hoses. I stuck out my hands and let the warmth wash the blood away. I walked up the still, empty hill holding my ear.

I broke up the gun and dropped the pieces in a storm drain. Some of them were shallow but some of them ran twenty feet down into the harbour silt. Some went all the way to China.

I found a taxi and climbed in. The cabbie asked where to and I said just drive.

III

Moment's Notice

Chapter 25

Outside, snow was falling on the trees. The tennis court was white. Narita Airport had closed. Buses trailed grey lines in the road. I bought teriyaki mackerel at the supermarket and Pokari Sweat from the coin-operated chiller in the hall and set it out on the window-sill so I could eat it with my hands. Children were playing tag in the night, running and slipping on the sidewalk. The air smelled like butcher's paper.

Bored, Candy once said. Bored by parties and lights and talking, you know?

Oh – I know.

The world used to be certain. Things were solid. Things weren't going to change. We had it licked. People could travel through space, fly faster than sound, fit a lifetime on a platter. We were intelligent, we were comfortable and we lived in a safe house. We could take anything, go anywhere and nothing could possibly go wrong, and we were bored because there was no loss in the world. And so to give our lives meaning, we brought loss to it.

I loved Alice because she felt that loss every day, as close as the tongue in her throat. Alice was gone, now. It took me a long time to work that out.

★ ★ ★

Auckland's power was restored by the end of summer. The police discovered the body in the car wash and assumed it was a gang hit: speed was big business, the gangs and importers jockeying for position. The story ran in all the papers, spooky tales about authority losing control.

I had dropped Helen Anyway's cell phone in the car. That piece of evidence put the dead man in her room. It was just enough for the police to chew on. They were still looking for me, but not as hard.

Lars put Lucy on a freighter. He got me a passport and a ticket on a Japan Airlines flight out of Christchurch. I shaved my head like a monk and left it all behind. But I did make him tell me where Candy had gone. I made him give me the number. He took some persuading. I had fucked up so many things now. I had a reputation.

He found her a position at the International Data Center in Maui, where she could listen to the French letting off nuclear bombs in the ocean, in the coral reefs of Mururoa. She was working with a team to compile event bulletins: seismic and hydroacoustic data. The army liked to push the button in the early morning so the chiefs back in Europe didn't have to stay up late. Candy sat around in beach shorts and the moonlight, waiting for the needles to jump.

The first time I called she talked to me for less than a minute. The second time I got a little more out of her. There was sand in everything. It jammed ball-point pens and the coffee machine. She had started to hate pineapple juice. She wanted to fly back to restaurants and the rain.

The bomb went deep. Wires broke the surf in tiny white whispers and dived into the green, the blue, the blue black: the limestone hole, six hundred metres down to a yellow metal case that waited, crouched in silence for the blink that told it to go off and kill itself. And each time she prayed for the compression area, the rock around the test zone. She prayed for limestone.

The ball-point pen was invented in 1938 by Laslo and Georg Biro. The fear of nuclear energy is nucleomitophobia.

On the last test the body-wave magnitude was metered at 5.5. Based on this figure the monitors at the University of Helsinki estimated the bomb yield at sixty kilotons. The French Nuclear Energy Agency confirmed Iodine 131 was found in the water around the atoll. Iodine 131 is radioactive and causes cancer. It kills people.

In 1945 after Fat Boy and Thin Man were built they were flown to the island of Tinian in the Pacific. Before the bombs were loaded, the scientists who had travelled with them from Los Alamos wrote on them with chalk: names, names of families, messages to the Emperor. Seventy-one thousand died in Hiroshima; forty thousand in Nagasaki. Victims for two and a half miles suffered heat burns. Tinian is north of Guam in the Marianas, to the east of New Zealand; Mururoa is to the west. Either side of us, like brackets. Little plutonium brackets.

We are all part of that history. We're surrounded by it. It doesn't matter where you think you are, because really, you're in the same place as everybody else: in the present, in the below where Candy's love and fear was tracking the bomb – the black, underground sun.

She spoke softly down the line, her breath rising and falling as gently as waves on black sand.

'I'm sorry I took so long,' she said. 'People are really terrible at taking messages. It's just whoever picks up the phone – you don't know if they'll write it down. Things are going crazy.'

'How long till the next one?'

'We never know for sure. We just set everything up and wait for the flash.'

A guy came up and asked her something and she broke off for a second.

'Sorry, Sam,' she said, coming back to the phone.

'Who was that?'

'You know what? I'm still learning their names. There are so many people here and they all come and go.'

'I'd like to see it sometime.'

'There's nothing to see. Just trees and a hut and the station. It's boring to look at, honestly.'

'I bet the beach is nice.'

'Yeah.' She gave me that. 'The beach is good.'

'Do you go swimming?'

'Yes.'

She couldn't wait to get off the line.

'So you heard all about it,' I said.

'I heard something,' she said. 'I knew what would have happened. I knew it would be bad but I didn't go and see him. I asked myself why not. It was weak of me.'

There was the faintest tremor in her voice, so subtle it could have been a trick of the connection.

'Jules didn't listen to anybody,' I said.

'All I remember about him are the things he forgot a long time ago. It had been over for a long time, Sam. I want you to understand that.'

The kids downstairs had gone inside. It was getting way too cold.

'I'm not in love with you, Sam.'

'I know.'

'You had me and I left. It's just in your head.'

'I thought you were maybe burning a bridge.'

'It just happened like everything else happened. All these things passing one after the other, like traffic. If I'd stayed it would have been the same thing over again. I was beating my head against a wall. I was getting nowhere. I had to move.'

It felt like Jules was still around and we were talking behind his back. Some people you never leave. You just don't want to watch them go.

'So you're all just sitting round, huh?'

'It's so quiet,' she said. 'The sea's flat and the moon is on the water and there are no clouds. It's really beautiful. And then in two minutes it all goes crazy.'

'What about your blade?' I said.

I heard her swap the receiver to the other ear.
'Candy?'
'Candice,' she said.
The test warning came through and she had to go.
Again.

I finished eating and had a shower and came out and lay back on the bed. My shoulder hurt. A handwritten cardboard sign by the phone advertised a full massage for sixty dollars, but the pain wasn't in the muscle: it was just beneath the flesh. Another piece of glass was coming through.

I turned on the TV. The weather on CNN had some shots of the snow around the city. The satellite showed a big front moving in. All connecting flights had been grounded. The government was warning travellers that there would be delays. Police and emergency services were on standby as a fine white blanket drew itself over the buildings and streets.

It was all over now – all of it. I closed my eyes. I was owed sleep from a long way back. I was owed time without dreams.